# WINCHESTER-THORPE SCHOOL FOR BOYS

BY

RICHARD C. ESLER II

Order this book online at www.trafford.com
or email orders@trafford.com

Most Trafford titles are also available at major online book retailers.

This book is a work of fiction. Any resemblance to real people, places
or events is entirely coincidental and unintended.

Note for Librarians: A cataloguing record for this book is available from Library
and Archives Canada at www.collectionscanada.ca/amicus/index-e.html

Printed in Victoria, BC, Canada.

ISBN: 978-1-4269-1856-8

*Our mission is to efficiently provide the world's finest, most comprehensive book publishing
service, enabling every author to experience success. To find out how to publish your book, your
way, and have it available worldwide, visit us online at www.trafford.com*

*Trafford rev. 10/29/2009*

**Trafford** PUBLISHING®   www.trafford.com

**North America & international**
toll-free: 1 888 232 4444 (USA & Canada)
phone: 250 383 6864 ✦ fax: 812 355 4082

# Dedication

This book is dedicated to my wife, Marion whose "whither thou goest" approach inspired me in my career.

# Dedication

This book is also dedicated to my father, Richard Esler who inspired me to write this novella.

# WINCHESTER-THORPE SCHOOL FOR BOYS

BY

RICHARD C. ESLER II

# CHAPTER 1

# BRADFORD

He slammed the front door of his house behind him and crossed the dark campus in long strides. As he entered the night-lighted corridor of Dawson Hall, he fumbled nervously for his office key. The loud click of the lock echoed sharply in the silence. In one motion he flung open the door, snapped on the lights, and with a last burst of anger kicked the wastebasket across the long spacious office.

"What the hell am I doing here?" he muttered to himself as he eased his long, lean body into the high-backed swivel chair at his desk. It was almost midnight, and he was tired, very tired. He thought about his days at Harvard where he had been an All-American swimmer; he had punished and even abused his body with the stress of competition, but he had never felt as drained as he did right now. He seemed to be on a treadmill of committee meetings, fund-raising dinners, trustee conferences, and faculty interviews. The insistent telephone was always shrilling in his ears, even when it was silent.

He brushed the thin graying hair from his high forehead, and his fingers traced the angular hawk-like features of his face, then covered his eyes as if to make the world go away. With his piercing eyes unveiled, he thought that he probably looked like a hawk; in fact, his students had even nicknamed him "Hawk". But now he felt less like a hawk than like its prey, a weakening victim.

He opened his eyes unwillingly and stared at the pile of unanswered papers, all addressed to James T. Bradford, Headmaster of the Winchester-Thorpe School for Boys. He smiled derisively at the fulsome sound of the school's name. He recalled the classic scene in the movie The Graduate in which Dustin Hoffman was welcomed back home by all the transparent people of suburbia, one of whom urged him to seek a career in plastics. He remembered his laughter at the skillful mockery of "plastic" middle-class values, but his smile faded as he realized that he had become part of that plastic world.

Bradford suddenly stood up in protest and announced loudly to the official silence, "I don't need or want all of this!"

His narrowed eyes looked beyond his oversized, polished cocobolo wood desk and surveyed the trappings of his career. The large overstuffed leather chairs positioned on the thick rich carpeting reminded him of a stuffy exclusive London club for retired cigar-smoking brandy-sipping Admirals and Downing Street statesmen. The portraits, in oils, of Messrs. Winchester and Thorpe, co-founders of the school, smiled mockingly at him.

"Those rich meddling old bastards," he mumbled as he though bitterly about the two men who, having donated two and a half million dollars for the new Science-Mathematics Quadrangle, had obnoxiously insisted that an unusually large bronze plaque eternalizing their names be placed on the cornerstone. Since that time they had regularly interfered in every decision about the school's curriculum, as if the bronzing of their names had conferred a god-like omniscience about all things human.

Bradford's glance rested for a moment on the autographed picture of Harry Truman whose influence had been one of the few honest forces in his life. Bradford had received a special award at Harvard for his exhaustive scholarly research of Truman's life and presidency. The work had inspired Bradford to seek a career in history teaching. Again he broke the heavy silence of the room, "All that I wanted to do was to teach history and to coach swimming, and now I'm doing neither, Goddamn it!"

As Bradford moved toward the long couch in the corner, he remembered Truman's famous comment: "If you can't stand the heat, get out of the kitchen."

"Maybe I <u>should</u> get out," he said aloud with a question in his voice. He had been trying to convince himself that he needed only a short rest to relax, calm down, but intuitively he knew that he was kidding himself. Over the years he had successfully masked his nervousness and quick temper by assuming a casual free-and-easy air which projected a sort of scoutmaster image, everybody's good guy. Few people remembered, he thought, an early incident in which, as a young History teacher at W-T, he had pounced raging on a stubbornly defiant student, dragged him with an iron grip out of the classroom, and then threw him crashing through a set of heavy double doors in Dawson Hall.

Bradford tried to put aside his anger with himself as he stretched out on the couch. He relaxed, but his thoughts tumbled through a circle of faces -- friends who were now enemies and enemies who were now friends and friends who were now gone. He stiffened as he pictured the departure of his predecessor from the Headmastership of Winchester-Thorpe. He imagined, in the dark shadows of the past, two shriveled spectres whose chalky faces kept solemnly repeating in sing-song unison,

"The Founders and Trustees of Winchester-Thorpe are no longer confident in your ability to administer the school and therefore respectfully ask for your resignation."

Was this a premonition of his own fate? Bradford's palms began to sweat with the fear that he too might be stripped of his responsibilities before he had the chance to renounce them with dignity. He didn't really give a damn about the title he held. He had gladly given to others much of his decision-making power. He had been somewhat insecure about his own abilities in fund-raising and budgeting, and the Board of Trustees had eagerly taken over these responsibilities with his blessing. His colleagues on the faculty had gladly assumed more and more of the work in supervising their departments and groups.

As Bradford drifted off half-asleep, he realized with a certain fatalism that his end was approaching; he had been slowly drained of his life's blood. He knew that both his friends and his enemies, they who had blended so indistinguishably in his dream, would soon be pecking at his carcass. "Gooddamn vultures," he mumbled as he sank into unconsciousness, and then deeper into a profound sleep.

# CHAPTER 2

# HUNTLEY

J. Robert Huntley III was pleased with himself, very pleased indeed. His small fat fingers moved deftly over the papers in front of him, and he officiously initialed the last changes in the school calendar for next year. He had worked tirelessly during the past two weeks but had carefully and successfully concealed his long hours from his friends on the faculty of Winchester-Thorpe. Everyone would marvel at the effortless way in which he had handled the complex job of creating a smooth coordinated schedule of classes, activities, and events.

He sat back in his heavy chair, relaxed for the first time in weeks. He licked his thick lips as a smile of satisfaction cut a wide line in the full beard obscuring his boyish moon face. His brown eyes sparkled with triumph. His wife Margaret would also be pleased, he thought. Huntley knew that she would greet him with a perfect porcelain smile, and her expensively manicured hands would offer him a chilled Absolut vodka martini prepared to his usual standard of excellence.

He remembered the day when he had brought home the triumphant news of his promotion to Director of Studies.

Margaret had tried to reward him in bed that night, but their mutual effort, as usual, had been like a sky rocket that fell over and fizzled out before it soared into the heavens. Oh, well, there was a great deal more to life than just sex. Both he and Margaret had prepared themselves for a brilliant success in the higher realms of society and educational administration. Oh yes, there would come a day. . . . Huntley's small moccasin-clad feet shuffled under his desk, pushing him away, and his searching hands dug into the tight pants pocket of his bluejean suit. His eyes glowed with delight as he pulled out a small brass key. This would unlock the hidden work of his secret ambition. He slowly opened the desk's private drawer and took out a stack of business cards printed in engraved Old English script on the heaviest of snow-white stock. The cards read:

J. Robert Huntley III, Headmaster
Winchester-Thorpe School for Boys

He savored the full impressive sound of the names, both his and the school's, an unbeatable combination. He felt that he was already in the final phase of his master plan. It wouldn't be long now. His carefully tailored lifelong dream was now about ready to unfold.

In his early days as an adolescent at Winchester-Thorpe, young Bobby Huntley was a soft chubby schoolboy who avoided his fellow students and lived a secretive existence. He regularly indulged in over-eating, especially sweets. He dressed sloppily, and he shunned any physical activity. He clung to his own small exclusive world and wanted no other inhabitants. He would hide in the library stacks, excusing himself from field trips and games. He was then free to roam the corridors of Dawson Hall and catch glimpses of the polished, private leather-bound office of the Headmaster. He remembered the day when he had been sent to that same Sanctum Sanctorum to explain

6

his conspicuous absence from a trip to the local zoo. Throughout the Headmaster's scolding, he had stared in secret delight and memorized the details of that rich decor. In childish fantasy he saw himself seated by divine right on the Headmaster's throne, monarch of all he surveyed. He carried that vision through the rest of his years at Winchester-Thorpe.

Huntley had been a brilliant scholar with a Grade Point Average of 4.0 and became valedictorian of his class. In his commencement address he welcomed his classmates to the real world while he himself secretly burned with the desire to return to this, his own and only world, a course which he would chart with unswerving and determined ambition.

When J. Robert Huntley III returned to Winchester-Thorpe as a Drama and English teacher, his credentials were excellent. He graduated cum laude from Harvard University, earned a Master of Arts in teaching from Johns Hopkins University, and performed with creative brilliance in a federally-funded arts enrichment program for the ghetto children of Baltimore. He wore the casual clothes and full beard of the young rebel, as well as an air of unpretentious but informed simplicity. His busy drone-like service in the school community won him recognition as a diligent worker among the students and his colleagues. Over the years he had crafted his solid image and had carefully disguised his vaulting ambition and wolfish cunning under a facade of casual competence.

The ladder to his success sometimes offered him the chance to climb more quickly than he had anticipated. After the completion of the Fine Arts Center, Huntley was appointed Chairman of Fine Arts. He recruited a sensitive painter for the drawing and design classes who turned out to be not only an excellent artist but also a teaching genius. Huntley also found a concert cellist who put together an innovative strings ensemble of surprising quality. Huntley also had a team of other superior teachers, and they together unwittingly painted a masterpiece of his departmental accomplishment.

He almost blushed when he recalled the rock concert, a clever promotional scheme which easily upped his popularity with the students and at the same time raised thousands of dollars for Winchester-Thorpe. After the noisy performance, the Fine Arts Center was a shambles of trash, discarded paper, empty drink containers, cigarette butts, and even ripped-off clothing. The blame was quickly shifted to the rock groupies from outside the school, the wild-eyed long-haired smoked-happy screamers.

Huntley's many projects and their successes, real or contrived, led to his appointment as the Head of the Middle School. There he initiated a blitz of new curriculum projects which cut across grade-level lines and combined fine arts with academic disciplines. Under the guise of individualized interest-centered learning, history surrendered to fort-building and noisy mock war games. The sound and sense of English were swallowed up in grotesque "camp" skits. The logic of mathematics was lost in a confused tournament of disorderly chess games. As a swelling avalanche of parental complaints threatened to bury Huntley's world of play-and-learn, he deftly stepped aside, and his loyal assistant was given the task of restoring order and reason out of the chaos, and shouldering the blame for the whole ugly mess, as well. J. Robert III, of course, survived and emerged as the brilliant and untarnished innovator.

Huntley was pleased but not at all satisfied with his present duties as Director of Studies. He knew that he could handle the job well; he was a good detail man, and his paper performances enabled him to live in his private world and to limit his contact with students. He longed to take the last step of his long climb to Headmastership. He was now ready to close in on his final victim whose removal would open a clear path to that longed-for office, the pinnacle of his career, where he would be as secure as God Almighty from the little lives around him.

"I am second in command," he spoke to the confining walls of his small office, "But not for long." His voice was determined, even ruthless.

# CHAPTER 3

# O'CONNOR

"You're in more fog than the Newfoundland Banks," he barked, his heavy jowls shaking like a gruff bulldog's. "Now that you've groped your way through number 1, try to score on number 2," he chided. "That's right. . right. . .okay. . .good job. . .you've got it," he said warmly.

His students furtively nudged each other as one of them was summoned, questioned and scolded privately, and then gently returned to the confidence of the group. Among themselves they called their teacher "Bulldog", but they knew that his barking was only part of the compelling art with which he drew them close to him. Respectfully, they yielded their minds to him, and he, in return, taught them with dedication and love.

John L. O'Connor, senior Master and English teacher at Winchester-Thorpe, paused for a moment and looked with soft gray eyes at his charges. They looked back at him with half-timid smiles. They had been well-prepared by their fathers and uncles for O'Connor's firm reign over their lives. His fame was legendary, and even the dullest youngster in the class could feel his teacher's confidence.

O'Connor treated his students with an iron-hand-and-the-velvet-glove approach, and they loved it. He skillfully mixed rough scolding with gentle praise, sharp criticism with inspired encouragement. Slowly but inevitably, an unshakeable bond grew between O'Connor and his students. He courageously upheld a tough standard of excellence and yet remained sensitive to the changing and often contradictory nature of their growth. John O'Connor was truly a master teacher.

He had first come to Winchester-Thorpe as a Latin instructor in the school's early days. This present term would mark his twenty-fifth year of unbroken service. That quarter century had passed swiftly, and he had witnessed many changes. He had watched with disappointment as Latin was transformed into Classics, a course with more history then language.

"Omnia Gallia est divida in partes tres" and "Arma verunque et cano Troyae" were lost in the detritus of yesterday along with their authors Caesar and Virgil.

When the dorm on the top floor of Dawson Hall was closed, O'Connor opened his large Victorian home to boarding students who still wished to live on the campus of W-T. He personally won the respect of the school community for his rigid standard of honesty and for the expectation of excellence which he imposed more strictly on himself than on his students. He made the honesty-plus-excellence code synonymous with the school; in the eyes of the alumni, parents, and students, O'Connor and Winchester-Thorpe shared the same identity.

A shrill bell punctuated the end of another lesson period. O'Connor walked with quick youthful strides down the familiar corridors. He was greeted with a constant chorus of "Good Morning, Mr. O'Connor" by the students, none of whom felt like a stranger to this seemingly ageless man. He disappeared through the door into his other world, the office of Head of the Upper School. He approached his administrative duties with his usual gruff but kindly manner and his honest high-performance goals. While he would roar at a boy for cutting classes, he never neglected to find out why and to counsel the student through the often intimidating life of the private school.

O'Connor's unqualified integrity and alarming frankness often made him controversial among his colleagues. He alienated some, especially those who had become envious of his status and influence. Other faculty members he sometimes took under his tutelage. One of these was James Bradford who learned to improve his teaching techniques and to control his hair-trigger temper. When Bradford had left W-T during his early teaching career to become Head of the History Department at Ashforth Academy, he enjoyed the reputation of a highly skilled teacher and a tolerant humanist, thanks to O'Connor's patient instruction.

O'Connor remembered well the decisive phone call which had insured Bradford's return to Winchester-Thorpe as Headmaster.

"Hello, Mr. Thorpe. This is John O'Connor calling."

"Hello, J.L. How goes the search for our new headmaster?"

"Well, sir, this is exactly why I called you. The faculty Search Committee met last night and unanimously recommended James Bradford as their leading candidate. You remember him, right?"

"I do indeed. What do you think of him, J.L.?"

"His recommendations are solid, and I know that he is a good man. Above all candidates, he knows our school well."

"That settles it," affirmed Thorpe decisively. "I'll call an immediate meeting of the Executive Committee. We need to move quickly to affirm the appointment."

O'Connor recalled how pleased he was with Thorpe's reaction. He looked forward to Bradford's return. He thought that Bradford, better than anyone else, could bring back under control those rebellious young teachers who mindlessly condemned anything old or established. The faculty was becoming increasingly louse-ridden with refugees from a rag-bag whom O'Connor privately called DDD's, meaning

Delapidated Degenerate Dimwits. These shabby sheep-like creature-teachers formed non-intellectual cliques to oppose all traditions, teaching methods, and school policies tried and proven by the past. Everything old was no good, and they said so quite openly. Some of them were a little more sneaky about it -- "Like that ambitious young egoist J. Robert Huntley III who needs to be stopped in his tracks," O'Connor said emphatically to himself.

After Bradford had returned as Headmaster and a term had gone by, O'Connor was disappointed. At the very beginning of Brad's tenure, he truly did bring new vitality to the school. His proposed changes had begun to push Winchester-Thorpe into the forward-looking 1970's. New buildings were planned, and the curriculum was being revised and activities updated. But Bradford was developing and exhibiting a high personal tension. He walked a tightrope between parents and students on one side and the faculty and trustees on the other. A flood of administrative details rolled in for his attention, and he soon allowed them to drown every minute of his long day. He became desperate in his frantic efforts to control the tide and please everybody. He even welcomed the trouble-making DDD's into his power circle. O'Connor was shocked, but he was most regretful about the change in his relationship with Bradford.

The new Headmaster repeatedly ignored any seasoned advice and at times even shunned O'Connor's presence. Bradford had apparently wanted to stand alone to face his new responsibilities. O'Connor was cognizant of the mounting pressures on Bradford and worried about the well-being of both his old friend and the school. He repeatedly tried to reason with Bradford.

"Brad, you've got to keep an eye on the machinations of the faculty."

"What do you mean?" snapped Bradford distrustfully.

"Some of them are out to cut your throat, and --"

"Bullshit!" interrupted Bradford, "They're all busy doing their jobs." He was apparently oblivious to the attitudes and ambitions of the teachers around him.

"The one who is the busiest chipping away at you is that deceptive wretch J. Robert Huntley III."

"For Christ's sake," said Bradford impatiently. "He's only trying to help me move this horse-and-buggy school ahead, not leave it behind the way it was in your generation!"

O'Connor recoiled, deeply hurt at the insinuation that he was militating against the progress of Winchester-Thorpe. He now knew sadly that Bradford would no longer listen to him.

Since that time, the relationship of Bradford and O'Connor had been reduced to an exchange of terse official memos. A wide gulf of silence separated them in the limited geography of the W-T world. O'Connor watched helplessly as the tide rose higher around Bradford and as he swallowed his problems. The relentless pressures of the Headmaster's job were pushing him under.

"He's going to fall," O'Connor predicted to himself with painful knowledge. He saw Brad's increasing nervousness and the surfacing of the high temper which pushed Brad into impulsive decisions. Bradford was losing control of both himself and the school.

"I must help him," said O'Connor to himself, "whether he wants it or not, before it's too late."

# CHAPTER 4

# THE FACULTY LOUNGE

Bradford stepped out of his office and turned down the corridor toward the Faculty Lounge. As he drew near, he heard the buzz of talk -- gossip, learned opinions, and probably political plotting. He knew that the conviviality would cease when he, the Headmaster, made his entrance. It did. He was greeted with icy silence. As he filled his coffee cup, he heard one squeaky voice say, "Good morning, Mr. Bradford." Young Bruce Linsley, the new cherry-cheeked French teacher, was making a clumsy attempt to ease the tense moment. Bradford turned around quickly and said in a distant tone, "Good morning, Bruce." Under his cold demeanor he hid his disgust and thought to himself, "The only one who even talks to me is the fuckin' fairy from Princeton."

As he left the lounge, Bradford sadly recalled an earlier time when he, as a young history teacher, met every morning with his gang of friends in that same room. "I used to be one of the boys, remember?" was his parting under-the-breath comment. A familiar scene from those older happier days repeated itself in Bradford's memory. In his mind's eye he could see the door of the Faculty Lounge burst open to frame the figure of Mario Costa, Director of Music at Winchester-Thorpe, who posed for a moment in the doorway. He dressed in a tuxedo and was holding up, a la Statue of Liberty, a square torch which looked deliciously like a box of fresh hot doughnuts.

"Yeah, Mario!" cheered the teachers, crowding around him to get their eager hands on the morning treat. He smiled in good-natured generosity and waited for the usual comments on his appearance.

"I'm glad our fat penguin made it through the night," quipped Rod Weston, the head football coach.

"I'll bet Mario ate all the holes," said somebody.

"Who the hell ever heard of penguins in Italy?" added another teasing voice.

"Mario, why don't you take a doughnut to the head, one with lots of sugar. He might give a ten-cent raise to such a sweet guy," suggested "Brad" Bradford, the new History teacher.

"And you could play "Winchester Cathedral" to him on your saxophone while he ate it," added Smitty, the debating coach.

Mario's many friends well understood that his tuxedo meant that he was just returning from an all-night playing engagement at a Houston night club. But they took great delight in teasing him, and he enjoyed it. A large reassuring hand patted him on the shoulder, and the booming voice of his old friend John Burns, Director of Athletics, said, "Your doughnuts are all gone, and you look like a French waiter with nothing to serve, but you're a good man, Mario."

Mario Costa was more than just a good man. He was a highly skilled professional musician and composer. He had mastered the saxophone at a very early age, and when barely seventeen years old, he won a place with the Stan Kenton orchestra. He loved the big band sound, but after five years the glamour of nightspots and concert halls had faded. Mario had grown weary of the traveling musician's bird-of-passage life style.

When he joined the Marine Corps, he spent his tour of duty as a member of the famous Marine Band. While he was stationed in California he was able to play also in Hollywood studio recording sessions for film sound tracks. After his release from the Marines, Mario had opted for college, studied music theory, mastered several other instruments, composed much original music, and eventually earned his bachelor's and master's degree in musicology.

When Mario Costa had first come to Winchester-Thorpe, he found that his great skills and wide experience had made him an almost magical teacher, and he soon created the school's first orchestra. Each year the students' musical artistry steadily improved until their playing was almost professional. Their annual schedule of concerts became the star events of the year.

Costa was not the typical tempermental maestro. He was modest about his success with the W-T orchestra and worried like a mother hen about each performance. He frequently warned his friends that this year's concerts would not be as good as last year's. However, at each event, the audience was awed by the polished playing of the school's orchestra. Mario Costa, like John O'Connor, demanded high performance from his students, and he taught them in the same manner -- with both sharp criticism and warm praise. His young musicians responded by playing to the height of their skills for their maestro.

When the Fine Arts Center opened, the orchestra staged a special entertainment to an auditorium packed to the doors with patrons. The chattering audience hushed as the house lights dimmed. A bright white spotlight suddenly flashed on Mario Costa and silhouetted the instrumentalists behind him. He wore a silver-threaded green formal jacket and flourished a long ivory baton. He bowed to the welcoming applause and led the orchestra into "Winchester Cathedral", their theme song. Costa reached for his saxophone and contributed an astonishing arpeggio which held the audience spellbound.

The spell was broken when a soft chuckle rippled through the crowd. Out of the right wing of the stage shuffled big John Burns the Athletic Director, clad in a suit of long red underwear and carrying a small straw suitcase. He stopped and faced the audience with the wide white-painted grin of a clown. His costume and make-up exaggerated his small head, huge shoulders and narrow waist. He was the perfect image of Bluto, Popeye's favorite villain. The laughter of the audience grew louder. .

Burns stepped behind Costa and tapped him on the shoulder. Costa turned around and in mock surprise said, "John, I told you, not tonight."

Very deliberately, Burns opened his suitcase and began to toss out rumpled cloths and dirty underwear. His searching hands finally came up with a small harmonica. He crowded past Costa to the microphone and blew one loud and very sour note. He then quickly repacked his suitcase, bowed to the audience, and stalked proudly off the stage. Mario Costa shook his head, turned to the crowd and said, "Ladies and Gentlemen, only at Winchester-Thorpe." The house thundered with applause and laughter. The rest of the concert was a succession of brilliantly played semi-classical and modern compositions in the fashion of the Boston Pops. One of the highlights was the performance of the new brass quartet made up of both students and faculty. Costa had worked long hours with them preparing for this night. When all was over, Mario and his musicians enjoyed a standing ovation of record length. The audience didn't want to go home.

John Burns was the sensation of the school. He received several student-inspired anonymous contracts from nonexistent Hollywood film companies offering him fabulous salaries. He endured an almost intolerable amount of teasing from the Faculty Lounge gang. But he took everything with his characteristic good humor. Like Costa, Burns enjoyed the attention.

John Burns' intimidating size and his booming voice did not represent his true nature. He was a surprisingly gentle person who loved children and understood both their physical and emotional growth. To older boys he was the macho man, the strong athlete, but one who tolerated only fair play and good sportsmanship. To the younger boys he was their protective big brother who never punished them unjustly, always listened to what they had to say, told them stories, and inspired them to do their best.

Before his arrival at Winchester-Thorpe, John Burns has spent his earlier career with the Y.M.C.A. organization in Illinois. As a boy, he was an active member who slipped easily into an instructor's position. He was subsequently promoted to the Directorship of the Y.M.C.A. in downtown Chicago. Although an exceptionally big man, he was an accomplished gymnast who moved with the grace of a great ape on the rings and parallel bars. When he came to W-T, he organized and trained the school's first gymnastic team. In a short time W-T was regularly placing high in regional gymnastic competitions among private schools.

Burns was at his best as Director of the Summer Day Camp at Winchester-Thorpe. Since the camp was open to other students besides the boys of Winchester-Thorpe, Burns insisted that the camp must accept girls as well as boys. He skillfully designed a summer program with an endless variety of games, creative crafts, swimming and diving classes, timber cruising, bird watching, outdoor cookery, botanical lessons, rock climbing, field trips, fishing parties, camp-outs, desert endurance days, wild animal studies, stream improvement work, conservation colloquies, cabin building, star mapping, and other fascinating activities. No aspect of youthful interest and intellectual curiosity was left out, and all the activities were pointed toward teaching physical skills, mental competence, spiritual confidence, and social cooperation. The counselors who worked for Burns were chosed for their patience and tolerance as well as their expertise. Many for them were former students who knew and understood the programs and purposes of the W-T Summer Day Camp.

Burns naturally jumped into the Day Camp activities with the youthful enthusiasm of a camper. At the swimming sessions the children screamed in delight as Burns did his famous cannon-ball dive which created the summer's biggest splash and turned the pool into a giant wave. Each pool-rat then swam furiously to be the first one to reach Burns and to "rescue" him from drowning. The younger children quickly lost their fear of water, and by the end of the summer camp they had all learned to swim with confidence.

On field trips Burns was both the campers' guide and the center of attention. At the zoo he usually carried one small camper on his shoulder and raised one with each arm so that they could see over the crowd. He was also surrounded by others who clamored for his attention, pulling at his sleeve to share with him the joy of their discoveries.

The campers looked forward to their overnight wilderness camp-outs. Some of them had never spent a night away from home or away from paved streets and urban atmosphere. Many had never cooked a meal over an open fire. After the meal was done and the over-blistered hotdogs and burnt toasted marshmellows were being happily digested, Burns gathered the children around the campfire and told them stories, fascinating but preposterously tall stories about himself and Paul Bunyan and his blue ox Babe who was ten yards and two pick handles from horn tip to horn tip; and how they worked on the railroad in Illinois, driving rail spikes with one blow of their 100-pound sledge hammers. The tales, of course, came strictly from Burns' vivid imagination and his reading.

But the youngsters were fascinated, and Burns took great delight in telling the Baron Munchausen stories.

At the end of each week the entire camp gathered for a program of awards. The "Broken Shoelace Champion" award was given to the camper who had the most knots in his tennis shoe ties. The "Luncher Cruncher Pig-out" award was given to the camper with the greatest appetite. The "Grubby T-shirt" prize was given to the crumb-bum with the dirtiest clothes. The "Snore More" trophy was given to the camper who was latest to get up in the morning. And then the "accomplishment" awards -- the "Longest Lap" badge for the beginning swimmers who struggled until they completed a lap of the pool; the

"Slugger" badge for softball players who finally learned to hit the ball; the "Cross Country" patch for those hikers who survived the 20-mile wilderness walk; and numerous ribbons for First Place, Second Place, Third Place, and Honorable Mention in a variety of art and craft contests. There was even a boy and girl selected to be King and Queen of Camp Concern because of their consideration for others.

The parents of the campers were pleased with their children's summer experience. Those who at first regarded the camp as a convenient baby-sitter suddenly found their offspring to be more self-confident, more willing to share in household chores, and much more considerate of their siblings and friends. Many children returned for more golden summers with their friend John Burns. The Summer Day Camp's excellent reputation not only reflected the quality of Winchester-Thorpe but also enhanced it.

Another of the Faculty Lounge regulars was Jerry Thomas, Biology teacher. He never quite made the early morning gathering. He frequently suffered from "the morning after the night before", having tippled and hopped from bar to bar after school hours. Thomas always appeared at the mid-morning break when the Lounge gang met to drink coffee and watch old Laurel and Hardy films. Thomas, like Mario Costa, usually made a dramatic entrance. With his rimless glasses perched on the end of his nose, he would lean his broad shoulders and muscular arms on the narrow yardstick he always carried, and he would break into a clumsy imitation of Charlie Chaplin's walk. He was greeted with uproarious laughter and a shower of pillows from the couches and chairs.

Thomas was not only a master biology teacher but also a brilliant botanist. Over the years he had collected thousands of tropical plants and flowers in the extensive greenhouse which he and his students had built themselves. Each year in the spring Thomas and his students took a field trip into Mexico to study and collect plants. He himself went far up the Amazon in Brazil every summer and lived with the primitives and thereby built up an unparalleled collection of orchids.

In fact, he had the distinction of discovering a variant of the emphytic tree-growing Spider Orchid to which the Internation Code of Botanical Nomenclature has given the name <u>Brassia caudata gigantus Thomas.</u> The longe slender tails of the sepals of this reare orchid grow to be 20 to 25 inches long, and the blooms look like families of super-spiders poised on a limb. Because of these and other such specimen plants, Jerry's greenhouse was a meeting place for the biggest names in today's botanical field.

When he was not ranging the rain forests somewhere, Jerry Thomas was exclusively interested in teaching his classes and working in his greenhouse. He scoffed at school politics and calmly disregarded school rules and regulations. He was particularly short-tempered with any institutional demands which kept him away from his work. When the Board of Trustees decided to add a planetarium and ob-servatory on the science wing, Jerry snorted, "show biz science," with scorn, When the former Headmaster told Thomas that he would have to tear down his greenhouse to make room for the planetarium wing, he flatly refused. On the same day he tendered his resignation to the Headmaster and Board of Trustees.

Mr. Thorpe, Chairman of the Executive committee, recognized Thomas's brilliance and tried unsuccessfully to persuade him to stay. His sudden departure shocked Winchester-Thorpe. The school had rejected many teachers in the past, but no teacher until Thomas had rejected the school. His friends understood his reasons for leaving, but the old faculty lounge gang had lost one of its stalwart spirits. Soon they were to read about Dr. Jerry Thomas's appointment to the faculty of a prestigious ivy league university where he occupied the Linnaeus Chair of Botanical Science.

Although Thomas was the first master teacher to leave, he was soon followed by John Burns. When the Board of Trustees suggested that the Summer Day Camp be replaced by a football camp, Burns, of course, vociferously refused. Mr. Winchester himself was father of the "suggestion" and, not by coincidence, was also father of a son named Hardin who was the star quarterback of the school's football team. After the Board insisted on eliminating the Summer Day Camp in favor of a shoulderpad-and-sweat session, Burns stormed like an angry elephant through the gymnasium equipment room and gathered up a dozen footballs. He packed them in a big box and enclosed a note to Mr. Winchester which made a pointed and crude suggestion about where he might stuff both the footballs and his summer program.

John Burns left immediately for Chicago where he rejoined the Y.M.C.A. and became Director of the International Y.M.C.A. Summer Camps Program which he administered from his Head Camp in the Wisconsin Dells.

Mario Costa was still lamenting the abrupt departure of his good friend John Burns when he was summoned to the Headmaster's office. He was handed a set of "strong recommendations" for restructuring his Music Department. These came from the Athletic Committee of the Board of Trustees, chaired by Mr. Winchester. Costa was told to convert his student orchestra into a large brass band with a unit of drum majors and a team of banner or flag wavers. These students were to be trained for intricate marching maneuvers so that they could provide 30-minute entertainments during the half-times at all Winchester-Thorpe football games, both at home and away.

Costa exploded into a long loud and emotional protest. He did not waste time on the Headmaster but went straight to the elder Winchester who was obviously trying to change the world in favor of his son Hardin.

"You, Mr. Winchester, the founder of this school, have devoted your life and your fortune to the best possible education for our sons. You would surely not require me to destroy one of our finest tools of culture at the time of its greatest popular achievement." Mario was building up to an oratorical pinnacle of protest. "You would surely not have us trade brass for Beethoven, of the tramp of marching feet for the sweet strains of violins and cellos, or the bass grunt of a sousaphone for the melodious harmony of a harp. We cannot commit musical suicide before our many patrons and benefactors." Here Mario injected a note of gallows humor -- "They would most likely want to use a Remington on any Winchester in their sight."

But Mr. Winchester was adamant. He insisted on the marching band at the expense of anything in the Music Department, including its Director.

Thereafter, Mario Costa shut his mouth. He opened it only to make one long-distance phone call to an internationally known Hollywood producer. Then Mario phoned the school to cancel his classes. He was never seen again in Houston.

During the following weeks, stories appeared in news service dispatches and national magazines about the musical genius who had become Vice President of Musical Production for the largest film maker in the world. Not a single work was published about Costa's antecedents at the Winchester-Thorpe School.

Officially, the school kept silent about the loss of the triumvirate of master teachers, hoping not to erode the W-T image of perfection. But the departure of Jerry Thomas, John Burns, and Mario Costa had cut the heart and spirit out of the faculty and much of the public presentations out of the school's schedule. Bradford, as the present Headmaster, worried about keeping up the educational strength and social influence of the school. He had hoped to revive and restore the basics, but he soon became too busy being the agent for minor changes and the solver of miniscule problems that his vision became narrowed and foreshortened. He understood that the school's strength depended directly on both the hard work and good will of the faculty.

He now sensed that the normal gripes of the faculty had taken on a critical razor's edge.

"Maybe O'Connor is right," he mused. "Maybe they're out to cut my throat."

# CHAPTER 5

# THE GOURMET SUPPER CLUB

O'Connor was right, and Bradford knew it. After Costa and Burns and Thomas were gone, and their auspicious influence with them, O'Connor watched the Faculty Lounge deteriorate into a club of malcontents. He did what he alone could do, but the teachers splintered into groups devoted to malicious gossip or to diatribes of discontent. Political cliques grew in strength and numbers. While Bradford was busy walking his tightrope, the faculty was secretly busy trying to knock him off the wire.

One of the most formidable cliques was the Gourmet Supper Club. The group originally began as a social gathering where teachers could smoke, drink, swear, and relax outside of the confines of Winchester-Thorpe. Now the group's purpose had become more political than social. It was not by accident that the club was five years old on the fifth year of Bradford's tenure as Headmaster. There were some who had been toasting his damnation from the very first.

The Gourmet Supper Club met every Wednesday evening at

different faculty homes. This latest meeting was important inasmuch as the guest speaker was Dr. Joseph Gibson, Chairman of the History Department. He was there to outline the idea of an instructional council as a means of organizing the faculty against the present administration, i.e. Bradford.

At the happy hour that evening, the olives were put away so that everyone would be drinking Gibsons (extra dry martinis with lemon twists instead of olives) in honor of the evening's speaker. And honor him they assuredly did. The vodka Gibsons flowed like a spring freshet, and the tongues wagged ever more freely.

"Nashur'ly you've heard the latesh," began one well-looped faculty member. "Bradford ish havin' trouble at home. Hish wife is hidin' in a bottle." He picked up a vodka bottle and emptied the dregs in his glass. "Can't be thish bottle. Mush be a shmall lady."

"No wonder," added a slightly more sober voice, "The dumb bastard is never at home. Too busy kissin' ass."

"I don't blame Betty," commented another teacher. "She was never cut out to be a Headmaster's wife. Too shy, doesn't like to entertain, hates to party."

"If he can not handle his domestic situation," pronounced Kenneth La Croix, a young English teacher, with drunken profundity, "it therefore follows that he will be unable to properly administer his school. Oh, shit! I've split an infinitive!"

"That's precisely the point. That's why we are here," another voice pronounced emphatically.

"To split infinitives?" mumbled La Croix in alcoholic wonder.

The conversation was interrupted by the arrival of Henry Prescott, defrocked Episcopal priest and tough-talking chaplain of Winchester-Thorpe. He was always a welcome member of the group.

He entertained them with stories of missionary work in Africa where he had lost an eye. He impressed them with danger-filled talks of his ministry to the street gangs of Laredo, Texas. Everyone remembered how he had introduced himself at a faculty meeting. He had told about an incident in which two young gang members had seen him one day on a Laredo street.

One boy turned to the other and asked, "Ain't that Father Prescott?"

The other answered, "Hell, he ain't no father. He's got six kids."

Prescott entered the living room and made the sign of the Cross with a vodka Gibson in a mock blessing of the meeting. He was greeted with inebriated laughter.

"How in... hell are you, Father?" asked La Croix with irreverent prophecy.

"God damned fine," answered Prescott with equal irreverence and prediction.

"Dominoes, Dominoes, cigarette butts, I can drink more than the two of us," sang an off-key voice in mockery of a Catholic chant.

Another teacher said, "Pas vobiscum, frater."

Prescott lifted up a finger. "And pees on you, too, brother."

The doorbell announced the arrival of the guest of honor, Dr. Joseph Gibson. Immediately equipped with a large glass of his namesake drink, he joined the celebrants for the rest of the happy hour which was waxing very very happy.

With Gibson attending, the gossip about Bradford resumed with renewed intensity.

"Bradford has been a little jumpy lately. Have you noticed?" asked La Croix. "Just the other day he chewed me out for throwing a little monster out of class."

"That clown has a lot of room to talk," Gibson said with sarcastic scorn. "You know, he used to teach in my department, and he was a real hothead. I still remember the day he picked up a student bodily and through him through the doors of Dawson Hall. The parents wanted to sue the school, and I took the heat for the whole damned incident. I had to practically get on my knees to the parents to get the whole ugly affair quieted down."

"There goes another infinitive, shplit again," mumbled La Croix, deep in his cups.

"I didn't know he was like that," said Bruce Linsey in naive amazement.

"Yes, Bruce, you don't know him as I do. You're still new here," commented Gibson. Lindsley was in his first year as the French teacher. He had felt lonely and lost, so he had joined the Gourmet Supper Club for social rather than political reasons.

"I don't think Bradford can handle the pressures of his job," "Father" Prescott wisely observed.

"You know what President Truman said," added Gibson. "If you can't stand the heat, get out of the kitchen."

"An' take all the shplit infinitives with you," said La Croix out of the depths of his vodka.

"I'll drink to that," Prescott concluded

A mellow musical chiming announced that dinner was ready. The gourmets flocked into the dining room, anticipating what they knew would be an excellent meal. Bruce Lindsley struggled to his feet and weaved unsteadily to his place at the table. There he discovered a glass of chilled white wine which he grabbed, half-spilled, and raised on high.

"I pro. . .pro. . . proprose a toast to our beloved school, Thinchester-Worpe, and' to the headbastard. . ."

Lindsley's thickened tongue stopped, his body teetered forward, his face ready to fall into a bowl of hot venison soup in front of him. Then his bones seemed to liquify, and he collapsed into a heap of old clothes on the floor.

"I knew that swisher couldn't handle his drinks," Prescott said. "Smitty, why don't you and Rod put him to bed. But don't climb in with him."

"Ass holes aren't my taste, padre," said shitty Smitty as he and Rod Weston lugged Lindsley out of the dining room. They returned immediately and sat down to a sumptuous repast:

Appetizer wine - Fume Blanc, Chateau St. Jean, 1988.
Hot venison broth with puff-pastry croutons.
Cocktail of Dungeness crab claws and clossal prawns with
    Horseradish sauce.

Khachapuri stuffed cheese bread.
Salad of artichoke hearts, Shitaki mushrooms, hearts of palm.
caperberries, ripe olives, and quail eggs on fresh spinach leaves
    with real Roquefort dressing.
Dinner wine - Cabernet Sauvignon, Clos Du Bois, 1987.
Prime ribs of beef au jus, very rare.
Yorkshire pudding.
White asparagus with lemon butter.
Dessert wine - Sherry, Tio Pepe - Fino, Gonsolez Byass,
Mousse au chocolat.
Crown Comice pears.
Prince-of-Wales double Gloucester cheese (Stilton & cheddar).
Circassian walnuts.
Rare Mandarin tea.

Gobbling the goodies did not prevent the group from going on with their favorite sport -- Bradford-bashing.

"Come on, Joe," prodded La Croix. "Tell us about your plan." The good food had banished La Croix's alcoholic haze. He was a young idealist who was always looking for a cause to champion. He also enjoyed the challenge of a good fight. That's way he had joined the Gourmet Supper Club and had become one of its most active members.

Dr. Joe Gibson began. "When I was assistant to the President of Syracuse University, I remember that the faculty organized the teachers into a council which formally presented a list of grievances and specific demands to the president. He was obliged to acknowledge their joint communication and to answer their demands rather than sloughing them off."

"It will never work at Winchester-Thorpe," Prescott pointed out. "Bradford doesn't have to answer to the faculty. He's in too solid with the Board of Trustees. Anyhow, he doesn't give a damn about the teachers. He's too hung up on involving the students in everything. Do you recall the last faculty retreat where he insisted on having students there? Christ, you couldn't drink, smoke, swear, or even breathe."

"Wait a minute!" exclaimed La Croix. "I've got an idea. Why don't we organize a Student-Faculty Senate? We can give the students enough rope to hang themselves and Bradford, too."

"Not Bad," commented Gibson. "Not bad at all. But who would present the proposal to Bradford? He doesn't trust most of us."

"What about our host?" suggested Prescott. "He's the only one around who's in like Flynn with everybody. By the way, where the hell is he? I need another glass of wine."

At that, the kitchen door swung open, and mine host stood in the doorway, equipped with a napkin-wrapped wine bottle and a broad smile. He was a study in white -- long chef's apron, buttonless chef's coat, tall tocque blanche on his head, and his teeth gleaming across the full beard covering his boyish moon-face. Here was none other than

J. Robert Huntley III.

"Anyone care for another small libation?" He rounded the table, removing the emptied salad plates and filling the second wine glass with the dinner wine.

His wife Margaret then emerged from the kitchen carrying a large silver tray heaped with inch-thick slices of blood-rare prime ribs of beef. Bradford-bashing was momentarily forgotten as the gourmets tore into the warm red meat with almost savage hunger. Their complimentary comments came thick and fast.

"Bob, How did you ever achieve this toothsome taste?"

"Why, I don't even need a steak-knife. I can cut it with my table fork."

"This is undoubtly the best prime rib I have ever tasted."

As the Yorkshire pudding and the accompanying au Jus gravy went around, the comments grew even more extravagant.

"I will never eat again. Any meal after this one would be a disappointment."

"The great chefs of Europe will have to step aside."

"This dinner elevates our supper club to the dizziest heights of gastronomy."

"Totally epicurean!"

Huntley looked on smilingly, but with a certain cool imperious arrogance. At the same time he took great delight in knowing that he had outdone the other hosts in providing the most lavish and savory spread for his guests.

Huntley was more than glad to carry the student-faculty senate proposal to Bradford. He knew that the Headmaster would be easily convinced of its value. Huntley smiled slyly as he thought how perfectly this fit his secret planning. It would reinforce Bradford's implicit trust of him, and he now had the complete confidence of his colleagues. He had successfully manipulated everyone around him and bid well to become the mastermind behind the scenes. Bradford's demise was now inevitable. Huntley licked his full red lips almost as if his ambition had made him powerfully hungry.

With his usual officious promptness, Huntley presented himself early the next morning at Bradford's office.

"Good morning, Brad. May I see you for a moment?" Huntley asked with his well-rehearsed casual comradely air.

"Sure," Bradford replied. "Grab a seat. What's on your mind?"

The Headmaster eased himself down behind his desk and reached for his coffee cup with a shaking nervous hand. He looked very tired. His usually piercing eyes seemed to be heavy and dulled from lack of rest. Huntley leaned forward in a confident I'm-your-best-friend attitude and in a low key said, "Brad, I think that some of the faculty want a greater voice in what goes on around here, and as you know, the students are asking for greater involvement in the decisions affecting the school. I have something in mind which will satisfy both groups."

"What's that?" asked Bradford with eager openness.

"I suggest that we eliminate the old student council and form a joint student-faculty senate," proposed Huntley with a triumphant smile.

"That's a damn good idea!" exclaimed Bradford. "Bobby, that brain of yours is always working overtime. The senate would have students and now -- suggesting, discussing, debating, deciding, agreeing, and promulgating all kinds of creative ideas for the betterment of Winchester-Thorpe."

"Would you like to organize and run the thing, J.R.?" suggested Bradford. I'm not a good committee man, and besides, I've already got too much on my plate, too damn many meetings to attend."

"I'd be glad to take over the project," Huntley agreed, and to himself he added, "and the rest of the school as well."

J. Robert Huntley III was again pleased with himself. Bradford had unwittingly played right into his grasping hands. Huntley stared at Bradford across the desk and imagined himself as a skillful big-game hunter who had his quarry in sight. He would fit his Winchester rifle against his shoulder, line up the prey in his sights, and soon he would choose the right moment to squeeze the trigger. Boom!! Bradford would fall out of that big chair behind that coveted desk.

## CHAPTER 6

# THE STUDENT-
# FACULTY SENATE

Bradford's memo to the faculty was as terse and this he sent to
O'Connor.

> To:    The Faculty of Winchester-Thorpe
> From:  James T. Bradford, Headmaster
> Subject: Faculty meeting
> A brief but important faculty meeting will be held on
> Wednesday, October 8, 1975 at 7:45 A.M. in the
> auditorium.  Please be prompt.
>
> J.T.B.

The Wednesday time period of 7:45 - 8:15 A.M. was regularly set aside
for faculty meetings.  However, such meetings were infrequent, and
the time was normally used as extra help sessions for floundering students.  This was also a way in which Bradford avoided long drawn-out

faculty meetings which he despised. He was already tired of the numerous committee meetings which required his attendance. He was beginning to believe cynically in the saying which described a camel as a horse put together by a committee. When he thought about the faculty as a "committee of the whole", it became a monster he didn't care to face.

Bradford's memo brought some caustic comments from the faculty:

"What in hell is Bradford up to?"

"Maybe he'll announce his resignation."

"Probably a vacation on the funny farm for Nerval Merval."

"I'll bet he died and left us a suicide note."

"No such luck. At least, not yet."

On Wednesday morning the faculty, bored, blank and bed-wrinkled, collapsed yawning into the auditorium seats. This was interfering with their badly-needed morning coffee. Bradford stood before them with Huntley seated at his right wearing a pasted-on smile.

"Good morning," Bradford began. "I would like to announce the formation of a Student-Faculty Senate which will replace our present outmoded Student Council."

The faculty remained passively silent except for the shuffling of feet and a sarcastic solo voice comment from the back of the room -- "Maybe it will replace the faculty, too."

"I have appointed J.R. Huntley as President of the Student-Faculty Senate," Bradford continued. "He has been both a student and a teacher here and knows our school well. Are there any questions or comments?"

Bradford's query was answered with utter silence. All seemed indifferent to the development except for John O'Connor who offered no public comment although his face flushed in anger. He muttered to himself, "Doesn't he know what he's letting us in for?"

"If there are no questions, the meeting is adjourned." Bradford spun on his heel and left by the side door.

O'Connor returned directly to his office, closed the door, and began writing an angry respose to Bradford's announcement:

Dear Mr. Bradford:

I strongly object to the formation of a student-faculty senate at Winchester-Thorpe. The body of teachers and the body of students have always been and should continue to be two separate organisms with differing functions and responsibilities within the school community. In the past we have already experienced the disaster of giving students authority which they are unable to handle.

In the 60's during your absence from W-T, the school gave in to student demands for greater involvement. As a result, an on-campus cell of the Students for Democratic Action was formed. The SDA promptly declared a "Destructuralization" of the school. The dress code and other social behavior standards were junked. Dirt, long hair, and ragbag camouflage clothes became the order of the day, along with greasy headbands and black armbands.

And, of course, you did not hear Karl (Marxie) Wolf's inflammatory speech in chapel announcing that God was dead and that the students should rise up in rebellion and take over the school. He was vague about what they should do then, but that's the failing of most revolutionaries. This incident led directly to the dismissal of your predecessor.

I don't even have to comment on your choice of Huntley for president of the senate. You have simply added more fuel to the fire of his ambition. That designing character is now one step closed to taking over your job. I fear for the destiny of Winchester-Thorpe as an institution of learning, and I am already beginning to wonder who is running this school, both now and in the immediate future.

Sincerely,

John L. O'Connor

The next day O'Connor received a reply. Bradford returned the same letter and added a note to the bottom: "I am running the school. Objection overruled. J.T.B."

With even more reins of power in his hands, Huntley raced noisily through the small world of Winchester-Thorpe, setting up a bureaucratic structure of committees and sub-committees which initiated a paper war of memos and directives equalled only by the Federal Civil Service Commission. The Executive Committee of the Student-Faculty Senate was made up of Huntley the chairman, young Hardin Winchester who had been the former president of the Student Council and who was now Secretary of the Senate, Kenneth La Croix the faculty representative, and Henry Prescott the chaplain.

Early in November at the first meeting of the Executive Committee, the discussion centered on possible programs and activities for the new Senate. Huntley sat quietly like a benign Buddha with a beard while Hardin Winchester spoke, asking, "Shouldn't the Senate start with a community service project? The Christmas time CANS program has been a long tradition with our school, and we could easily involve the whole community."

"That's good," observed Father Prescott. "It's getting damned difficult to ask people around here to give. The program needs more attention."

The CANS program had begun many years ago and was a quiet collection of food, clothing, and Christmas gifts for the needy families of the local parish of the Episcopal Church. Donations by students and faculty were entirely voluntary and were gathered during the final week of classes before the Christmas Holiday. CANS was originally Father Prescott's idea, so he was glad to see it given new life by the Student-Faculty Senate.

Armed with his burgeoning authority, J. Robert the Third (O'Connor elided the "h") initiated an all-out no-holds-barred effort to win the popular support of the entire school community. His Madison Avenue touch transformed CANS into CANPAIGN-75!

It quickly took on the loud brassy fervor of a political rally. Overnight the school cafeteria became the Canpaign-75 head-quarters. Screaming posters covered the walls -- GIVE TILL YOU HURT, BURT -- DIG OUT YOUR DOLLARS, SCHOLARS -- A GIFT OF YOUR MONEY MAKES CHRISTMAS TIME SUNNY -- I CAN, YOU CAN, WE CAN, SO THEY CAN HAVE A CANFUL OF CHRISTMAS CHEER -- BUY A CAN, MAN -- GIVE IF YOU CAN OR EVEN IF YOU CAN'T -- CANTA CLAUS NEED YOU! -- Can Christmas be as good as you talk it? YES, If The Bread Comes Out Of Your Pocket! DIG THAT CRAZY LOOT, BRUTE -- THINK OF THE KIDS WHEN YOU YELL OUT YOUR BIDS -- HAVE A CANNY CHRISTMAS WITH CANPAIGN-75.

The next day O'Connor went to the cafeteria to have a quiet lunch with his colleagues. As he opened the door, a blast of heavy rock music hit him in the ears, and two dazzling spotlights, one red and one green, were alternately flashing on a pile of canned goods on the table by the door. His stunned eyes surveyed the cheap garish posters stuck on the walls and even on the ceiling. TEACHER, TEACHER, DON'T BE GREEDY, REACH FOR A BUCK AND HELP THE NEEDY -- NO MORE HAMMIN', FIGHT THAT FAMINE -- GET OFF YOUR CAN AND GIVE -- MOOLA, MAESTRO, PLEASE -- PROFESSOR, PROFESSOR, CAN YOU DIG IN A FLASH OUT YOUR OLD WALLET AND GIVE UP SOME CASH?. . .

O'Connor stared for a moment at a patriotic poster of Uncle Sam whose bearded face had been replaced by that of J. Robert Huntley III. His finger pointed mockingly at O'Connor, and underneath were the words UNCLE CAN NEEDS YOU! The noisy crowd around the auctioning table almost deafened O'Connor. Hardin Winchester stood on a platform, holding a box of pizza in his uplifted hand. Behind him was a huge poster -- CANPAIGN-75, HELP US BRING IT OFF, PROF.

"What do I hear for this delicious delectable succulent pizza with 10 toppings, all hot and ready to eat out of the ovens of Marco's Pizza Parlor?

"1.50," replied a small voice.

"Boo," jeered the gathering crowd.

"Do I hear $5.00?" Hardin was trying to stimulate the bidding.

"$10.00," shouted a voice.

Then the bids came in rapid succession. "$15.00."

"$20.00."

"$25.00."

"I have 25, I have 25. 25 dollars going once, 25 dollars going twice. . . Sold! For 25 dollars!"

Ian Sunderland-Smith, one of Hardin Winchester's classmates, had won the bid. He stepped forward with a bulging wallet and nonchalantly peeled off twenty-five one-dollar bills., Sunderland- Smith enjoyed flaunting his money. His family's wealth came from its vineyards and wine-making business; they were very rich, even by the degrees of wealth represented by other families whose sons attended Winchester-Thorpe.

O'Connor, who was not in the habit of public cursing, angrily confronted Hardin and shouted, "What the hell is going on here?"

"It's okay, Mr. O'Connor," Winchester answered. "Mr. Bradford approves."

"Well, I don't!" snapped O'Connor. He stormed out of the cafeteria and stalked back to his office. Immediately he grabbed paper and pen and dashed off a note to the Headmaster.

Mr. Bradford:

I am completely opposed to "CANPAIGN-75". What was once a school tradition for a quiet and tranquil climate conducive to study and learning is being destroyed by a raucous vulgar commercial exploitation of the worst kind. The school cafeteria has been turned into a carnival tent with our students acting as brassy barkers. I already know who is the behind-the-scenes ringmaster of this circus. In fact, his picture is on the wall down there, and it says he wants <u>YOU</u> (That part is true enough).

We already have enough reminders of material wealth in our school community. We do not need to endorse this crass display of bad-taste materialism. This kind of activity denigrates the dignity of our school and inevitably cheapens our image.

John L. O'Connor

This letter came back as usual, but this time Bradford was dodging the responsibility --

"Express your opposition directly to J.R. Huntley and the Senate. It is their program."

J. T. B.

O'Connor knew that any attempt to change, redirect or tone down CANPAIGN-75 would be as futile as trying to stop an avalanche or to abolish ice cream. So, the old lion stayed in his den, licking his spiritual wounds.

The second phase of CANPAIGN-75 was even more flashy than the first. With unbridled enthusiasm, Huntley decided to take the Christmas time appeal beyond the walls of Winchester-Thorpe into the surrounding residential community. The school's printing press cranked out hundreds of leaflets, and another bureaucracy was born; Huntley organized teams of students and teachers to distribute the leaflets and to follow up with door-to-door solicitations.

Inevitably and for the first time in W-T's history, academic work took a back seat to the busy activities of CANPAIGN-75. With reckless abandonment of their normal responsibilities, both students and teachers scurried about in response to Huntley's elaborate plan of canpaign. Nobody seemed to care about homework left undone or classes cut. Nobody, except John O'Connor. His protests fell on deaf ears. CANPAIGN-75 had absorbed everyone's attention, and it gathered the momentum of a speeding train.

In December, Huntley came up with the climactic event of the canpaign. He organized a competition in which the different classes would vie with one another in raising the most money and collecting the greatest number of cans containing food. Hardin Winchester especially liked the idea and knew that the money from his well-funded classmates such as Ian Sunderland-Smith would make the Senior Class an easy winner.

Immediately, the contest among the classes took on the fierce competitive feeling of rival football teams. The hottest of these internecine wars was between the Seniors and the Freshmen. Hardin, and

Ian and their crew threatened the collection efforts of the Frosh workers with Maffia-type intimidation, warning them away from the best prospective sources of donations. The younger boys responded with almost intolerable taunts and insults, trying to drive the Seniors to the physical violence which would get them disciplined.

Every school activity was marked by CANPAIGN-75. Most of the daily classes now imposed an admission charge of one can of food. Concerts, entertainments, and special events also had CAN charges. And even the daily morning chapel service which required personal attendance. The back of the chapel looked like a warehouse with boxes of canned food stacked to the ceiling. The students' weekly allowances were hit and a percentage gouged for the Canpaign. Ian Sunderland-Smith came through as expected and contributed five crisp one hundred dollar bills to the Senior Class which almost insured its victory.

For the final triumphant ceremony to wind up CANPAIGN-75, a giant Christmas tree was erected in the center of the chapel, and mounds of colorfully wrapped gifts were heaped under its branches. The trimming of the tree itself was reserved for the final assembly of the year which would mark the end of CANPAIGN-75 and the beginning of the school's Christmas vacation. Prez Huntley was busy preparing for that gathering. He knew that the entire school community would be there, even the most reluctant dragons of the faculty, and he wanted to make the ceremony as spectacular as CANPAIGN-75 itself. He had arranged for press coverage by the local newspaper. To add a Christmas-cherub touch to the celebration, he hired the boys from the first grade of a nearby elementary school to make ornaments and trim the giant tree. He even bought button-down Oxford-cloth white shirts and gray slacks for every little cherub so that their clothing would match the uniforms of the Winchester-Thorpe students.

One the day of the final assembly, the chapel was packed with faculty, students, parents, and alumni. The crowd spilled over into the aisles where they stood elbow to elbow. The very walls seemed to bulge. The air was tense with high-pitched excitement among the students as they waited for the results of the class competition in CANPAIGN-75.

The organ music of "Hark The Herald Angels Sing" hushed the crowd. The little boys paraded down the center aisle wearing the uniform of Winchester-Thorpe and carrying their hand-made tree ornaments. Their flushed cheeks and dazzled eyes gave them an angelic look, capturing the hearts of all who watched. The Seniors followed immediately behind the little ones and upon reaching the center of the chapel lifted the boys onto their shoulders so that they could reach and trim the upper branches of the big tree. By the time the trimming was finished, there was not a dry eye in the house.

The Seniors took their place in the front of the chapel, standing behind Headmaster Bradford, Huntley, and Father Garcia. The priest headed the local Episcopal parish and was there to receive the gifts and canned food for his people.

Bradford approached the microphone and said only. "Ladies and Gentlemen, I want to introduce J.R. Huntley. Chairman of CANPAIGN-75."

The crowd broke into loud applause. The students cheered and whistled in anticipation of the class competition announcement. The camera of the local press clicked and flashed. J. Robert Huntley III stood before the throng, smiling hugely through his beard and raising his hand as if in benediction. He was thinking to himself -- Bradford is really slipping; he didn't even welcome this crowd, didn't say anything to them, as a matter of fact, okay, good, this gives me a chance to grease the skids a little . . .

"Ladies and Gentlemen, worthy colleagues, respected alumni, students of our great school, and all of you good people who support and join us in our Christmas time celebration -- welcome! Welcome! Welcome one and all! This is a joyous occasion. We are happy that you could be with us in our attempt to express the true spirit of Christmas. This is what CANPAIGN-75 has been all about. This is the season for giving, for extending a hand to those less fortunate than ourselves, for being humble for our blessings. Let us be thankful for everything which falls upon us from on high.

I want to thank personally all the wonderful people who made CANPAIGN-75 a resounding success -- Students, teachers, merchants, townfolk, and our generous alumni. Our class organizations have worked especially hard in this humanitarian effort. I take great pleasure in announcing the winner of the class competition in CANPAIGN-75. . ."

Huntley paused dramatically in the breathless hush which suddenly fell on the audience. . ." The winner of CANPAIGN-75, with a collection of 65,000 cans and 35,000 dollars, is. . ." He paused again. Everyone leaned forward, and the seniors shuffled their feet and swelled their chests confidently, ready to leap up with a triumphant roar. . ." The winner is the Freshmen Class!"

For a moment, the Seniors sat in stunned silence, trying not to believe what they had just heard. The Freshmen yelled and whooped with delight, relishing their victory over the arrogant older boys. One of them laughed very loud and pointed a mocking finger at the crestfallen Seniors. It was the freshmen Vincent Campbell, Jr. who knew that he was largely responsible for the vistory of his class. At the last minute, he had persuaded his father, an heir to the Campbell Soup fortune, to contribute 20 cases of tomato soup and 2,000 dollars.

The Seniors were outraged at this unexpected turn of events. They all raised their fists in protest and shouted, "Down with the weenies!"

In one swift mob motion they poured out like a giant wave into the crowd, and the freshmen retreated, pushing back everyone in their way. People were jammed against the huge Christmas tree. It began to wobble and totter. The chapel seemed to swell like a balloon with the shifting shoving mob of people. Suddenly the side doors crashed open, and the crowd squirted out into the campus. They were just in time; the tall tree rocked past the point of no return and smashed to the floor, narrowly missing the last of the panic-stricken persons pushing to the exits.

Bradford and Huntley, and Father Garcia stood by helplessly and watched the disaster, hoping that nobody would be trampled. After the crowd cleared out, the chapel was in shambles, and CANPAIGN-75 came to a very inglorious end. However, the press coverage of this riotous event saved Huntley and the school from embarrassment. The next day's newspaper headline read: WINCHESTER-THORPE CAPTURES THE TRUE

SPIRIT OF CHRISTMAS. Not a word was mentioned about the riot and the destruction of the Christmas tree.

With the help of this kind of selective reporting, the school quickly focused on the successful results of CANPAIGN-75. Huntley emerged as the hero of the day. Everyone, barring John O'Connor, conveniently forgot the disrupted classes, the neglect of learning, and the Mafiosa tactics of the fund-raising. The Headmaster ignored the complaints of certain nearby townspeople who had refused to give to CANPAIGN-75 and had found crude red swastikas painted on their front doors. Everyone embraced the Machiavellian philosophy of the end justifying the means. Once again, Winchester-Thorpe retained its image of perfection and closed its walls to the outside world.

# CHAPTER 7

# THE GREAT TRAIN RIDE

Even after the lapse of the Christmas vacation, Winchester-Thorpe was still fired up with the high (and non-academic) spirits ignited by Canpaign-75. So Huntley and the new Student-Faculty Senate immediately went to work on their second project to fuel the scholastic furnace.

This time, Hardin Winchester not only came up with the idea but also provided the means with which to carry out his plan. He wanted to honor the basketball team, the best in the history of the school, and he looked forward to the championship game against Cunningham Collegiate School, Winchester-Thorpe's long-standing archrival. He again saw the perfect opportunity to unite the school and maintain its heightened spirit.

Hardin suggested that the school lease a train and transport the entire student body to Cunningham Collegiate for the big basketball game. Mr. Winchester, Hardin's father and co-founder of Winchester-Thorpe, had generously agreed to provide the funds for the project. He had been pleased with Canpaign-75 and was happy to sponsor the train ride. Huntley quickly seized the chance to create another spectacular event. In honor of Canpaign-75, he named the new project THE CANPAIGN TRAIN TO CUNNINGHAM.

The CANPAIGN TRAIN set the whole school ablaze with instant enthusiasm. Once again, Huntley fired up his bureaucracy to plan and organize the great train ride. And once again the school cafeteria became the spiritual center for the students. Just inside the door was a shrine made up of a gilded basketball with baby spots flashing off and on, bathing it in golden glory. The walls again shrieked with garish signs. One very large poster featured an Uncle Sam whose face was that of J. Robert Huntley III; he was pointing a long finger at the viewer and saying, "UNCLE WIN WANTS YOU". Other signs read:

CRUSH CUNNINGHAM
WE'LL MAKE A MESS OF C.C.S.
MAKE CUNNINGHAM OUR CABOOSE, MOOSE
SHINE OR RAIN WE TAKE THE TRAIN
MENU FOR THE BIG GAME:
Scrambled YEGGS and Cunning HAM
TAKE THE CHOO-CHOO
TO THE C C S BOO-BOO
HICKORY, DICKORY,
WE RIDE TO VICTORY
WINCHESTER-THORPE --
THE LITTLE ENGINE THAT COULD

An improvised student rock group called The Winchester Repeaters made a recording of "Winchester Cathedral" which had more noise than the "1812 Overture". It banged, blasted, and thundered in the cafeteria until the very walls trembled. Between pep rallies, train trip tickets were distributed to students, and sign-up lists were made up for the various cars of the train. Hardin Winchester insisted that one car be reserved for the exclusive use of the seniors. The rest of the student body could crowd into the remaining cars.

Huntley was meticulously thorough in his preparations for the train ride. He arranged for the club car to be stacked with cases of soda pop for the students and club soda for the faculty. He persuaded Bradford to donate food for the excursion from the school cafeteria and the cooking staff to prepare and serve it in the dining car. The brass section of the school's orchestra would provide musical entertainment in the club car. Huntley also rented an entire motel for the overnight stay in the town where Cunningham Collegiate School was located.

On the CANPAIGN TRAIN's day of departure, classes were dismissed early, and the student body assembled in the auditorium for a final pep rally. A huge banner stretched across the curtains of the stage, carrying the message in blood-red letters -- CRUSH CUNNINGHAM. The basketball team, flanked by

Headmaster Bradford and Huntley of the grinning beard, stood on the stage and faced the noisy crowd. Spontaneously, the students began to stomp their feet and yell, "KILL CUNNINGHAM" and "WE'RE NUMBER 1". With cheers and fight-songs they worked themselves into a frenzy. When the rally ended they exploded out of the auditorium like an angry mob and shoved their way into the fleet of buses which took them to the train station.

At the station, another mob scene occurred as the milling throng pushed, shoved, and jammed into the railroad cars. Huntley, Prescott, and La Croix were waiting on the platform to help the students board their designated coaches. In the confusion, no one noticed Ian Sunderland-Smith surreptitiously load some cases aboard the car reserved for seniors; the labels on the sides of the wooden boxes were covered with wrapping paper. When the platform was clear, Father Prescott and La Croix boarded the club car and became the official chaperons of the CANPAIGN TRAIN TO CUNNINGHAM.

The basketball team was sequestered in the rear of the last coach, supervised by three faculty members -- the Athletic Director, the Basketball Coach, and the assistant coach. Huntley, of course, chose not to go along on the trip, thereby insulating himself from any problems and contretemps which were bound to occur in handling such a large mob of students.

As the train pulled out of the station, hundreds of yelling youngsters waved their arms out of the windows like soldiers on a troop train headed for war. The seniors' car was draped with the bloody banner which had hung in the auditorium for the pep rally. The message CRUSH CUNNINGHAM rippled in the breeze as the brass band, which called itself "Thorpe's Corpse", blared and oompahed and thumped out their New Orleans hotlick jazz version of the saints-marching-in song, except that they had changed the lyrics to "When the Wins come dribbling in". And so the whole entourage sang itself into the sunset.

Inside the senior car, a group gathered around a table. Ian Sunderland-Smith was the center of attention as he pulled a fresh deck of playing cards out of his pocket. "Anyone for seven-card stud?" he asked. Every player put a dollar in the pot, and the poker game began. With each hand the stakes increased.

Suddenly, Sunderland-Smith put down his cards and stood up. "Excuse me a moment," he said as he left the table and went to the communicating door of the car to make sure that it was locked. When he returned, he broke into an imitation of W.C. Fields and intoned, "And now, Gentlemen, for a small libation." His outstretched hands held a bottle of champagne marked with his family's label. "Never play cards without champagne," he added.

Hardin Winchester interrupted and said, "Wait a minute, Ian. Maybe the champagne isn't such a good idea."

"Why not?" answered Sunderland-Smith. "Who's going to find out about it?"

"Bradford wouldn't approve of our drinking on a school trip," cautioned Hardin.

"But he's not here to stop us," Ian answered. "Anyhow, he'd let the students do anything."

"Yeah, he's a real pussy, all right," added another voice.

"What about the CANPAIGN?" commented another member of the group. "Didn't we get away with everything we tried?"

"Hell," said someone else, "Bradford couldn't object to the CANPAIGN. His loyal assistant Huntley handled the whole thing."

Hardin observed, "Some loyal assistant! Bradford doesn't know it, but Bobby the Beard is out to get his job. I know. I worked with Huntley. He's a smooth politician."

"It takes one to know one," said Ian.

"Shut up, and drink your bubbly," snapped Winchester.

Sunderland-Smith uncorked the first of many bottles of champagne, and the seniors toasted everything and everybody -- the school, the team, the coach, the great train ride, the Headmaster (with boos), the Archbishop of Canterbury, the Pope, the President, Miss America, and Canpaign-75. After these 10 toasts, Ian struggled to his feet once more and said in a slurred voice. "I propose a toast to the next headmaster of Winchester-Thorpe, J. Robert Huntley III, long may he wave."

"You're probably right," agreed Winchester.

"Who gives a shit? We won't be here to see it," added Sunderland-Smith.

"Cheers to the Class of '76," shouted the seniors as they drank another toast. The bubly flowed like buttermilk, and the poker game continued as the CANPAIGN TRAIN TO CUNNINGHAM sped on to the rival school. A buffet dinner was dished out in the dining car, so everyone was well-fed by the time the train arrived at Cunningham. Buses were there to transport the students directly to the gymnasium since it was about game time. The seniors had recovered their equalibrium enough to hide their indulgence and were chewing sen-sen like mad to disguise their bubbly breath.

The Cunningham Collegiate team proved easy to crush, kill, smash, murder, trample, or otherwise reduce to primeval dust. Winchester-Thorpe won the big game 72 to 39 in an uninteresting contest which proved that they were really Número Uno. The local police herded the excited students away from the school buildings and on their way to the motel where they were to stay overnight before their return train ride to Winchester-Thorpe in the morning. The seniors made a detour to the station and boarded the silent coach clandestinely. Each emerged with a bottle of champagne concealed under his jacket, and they proceeded to their motel suite for an all-night victory celebration. Father Prescott and La Croix, after checking that all students were inside, closed the door of their own room and had their own party.

The next day, the CANPAIGN TRAIN TO CUNNINGHAM trundled home without incident. The project was heralded as a brilliant success. The students, especially the seniors, returned to their classes with quiet confidence and immediately went hard to work on their studies with a suspiciously serious attitude. Bradford worried about the hushed dedicated manner of the older students. He sensed that something was wrong. He braced himself in a calm which seemed to presage a storm. It was as if the students were keeping some dreadful secret from him. They were. The disastrous news hit Bradford and Winchester-Thorpe in the form of a long angry letter accompanied by a bill of particulars from the owner of the motel where the students had stayed overnight:

LA FIESTA INN
"For Fun In The Sun"
Gordon LaLime, Innkeeper

January 20, 1976

Mr. James T. Bradford, Headmaster
Winchester-Thorpe School

Sir:

I regret to inform you that the overnight stay in La Fiesta Inn by the Winchester-Thorpe students resulted in very extensive, and very expensive, damage to my motel.

The greatest amount of vandalism and wanton destruction took place in the de luxe wing occupied by the seniors of your school. Room doors were kicked in, their locks and hinges broken. Tarzan-like antics on chandeliers had pulled them down from the ceilings. Carpeting was spotted with cigarette burns and chewing tobacco spit and ruined where students had urinated in the corners of some rooms. The initials "W-T" were brutally carved on lamp tables and kitchenette sink-tops. Mirrors were broken, and those left intact were defaced with obscenities written in shaving cream. Commodes were broken from impact with champagne bottles, and one was clogged with tennis shoes and had been overflowing all night. Two medicine cabinets where ripped off the walls. The stench of spilled wine and vomit and heavy blue smoke will require scrub-cleaning and fumigation of the entire wing.

Rooms occupied by the basketball team and coaches were left in good order, but the rooms in the rest of the Inn where your lower grade students were housed were badly damaged. Doors, walls, and even ceilings were spray-painted with profanities, the 4-letter word beginning with "F" appearing everywhere. Rooms decorated with tropical-design wall covering were used as blackboards, and porno pictures were drawn on them with indelible felt-tip markers.

Wads of bubble gum were tramped into the shag carpeting. Mattresses were soaked with red pop and urine, and the beds were full of corn chips and salsa drippings. A bonfire of toilet paper had been burned in a tub, and the ceramic tile scorched and cracked.

Windows were broken.

Outside, the pool area was left in shambles. Lawn chairs were tossed into the swimming pool, and liquid soap containers from the rooms were emptied into the water, creating soap suds which covered the surrounding grass and clogged the drainage system.

The whole revolting spectacle is the worst damage anyone has ever seen. The entire community is incensed over the destructive behavior of your undisciplined students. Winchester-Thorpe will no longer be welcome in our town.

I am attaching a bill of particulars which affords you an estimate of the approximate cost of restoring La Fiesta Inn. I will be billing you for specific amounts as the restoration proceeds.

I do not know as yet how many rooms will be out of service for how many days. The loss of income will be determined by day-to-day room requests and vacancies during the time required to restore the Inn. I will advise.

Yours regretfully,
Gordon LaLime

### RESTORATION OF LA FIESTA INN

| 13 Items | Estimated Costs |
|---|---|
| Replace 6 doors & hardware | 900.00 |
| Replace 2 chandeliers & wiring | 250.00 |
| Replace carpeting in 10 rooms | 5,600.00 |
| Replace 5 lamp tables & 2 sink-tops | 1,100.00 |
| Replace 4 mirrors & 3 windows | 540.00 |
| Replace 2 medicine cabinets & wiring | 90.00 |
| Replace ceramic tile, 1 bathroom | 75.00 |
| Redecorate & paint 14 rooms | 1,400.00 |
| Replace 3 double mattresses & bedding | 600.00 |
| Scrub-clean & fumigate all rooms | 500.00 |
| Drain, clean, & refill swimming pool | 500.00 |
| Clear & clean all drains & plumbing | 300.00 |
| TOTAL ESTIMATED COST | $12,355.00 |

Bradford was stunned. For a moment he stared at the letter without moving. How could the boys of Winchester-Thorpe act like a gang of inner city hoodlums? He was shocked and deeply hurt by their unconscionable behavior. He covered his eyes with his hands as if to hide from the reality of the present. Is this what I get for trusting students? Or for that matter, my own faculty? Where in hell were the chaperones while all this was going on -- Father Prescott and La Croix? Those pseudo-intellectual knee-jerk liberals probably locked themselves in their room with a bottle of single-malt Glenfiddich, convincing one another that it was psychologically beneficial for students to work off their high spirits.

His hurt suddenly changed to anger. He could feel his face heat up as his quick temper flared. In one motion he jerked his hands from his face, and his long arm swept across the top of his desk, scattering everything into a crashing disarray on the floor. Goddamn kids! Stupid fuckin' faculty!

Bradford stood up and looked at the scattered mess of papers, letters, pens and pencils, schedules, reports, in-and-out rack, paper clips, ink stand, and a dripping coffee cup. His glance shifted to President Truman's picture. At that moment Bradford began to understand the heat and weight of crisis responsibility which the President must have experienced so many times.

He slumped in his chair, exhausted from his outburst. He was alone in his hour of crisis. No use looking for someone else to share the responsibility. It would be great to quit, to walk away from this whole ugly mess. But no. He had to face the music. Nobody else. Just he alone. He thought about others who were involved -- Huntley, of course, who was nowhere to be found at that critical moment. Come to think of it, our bearded Bobby seemed to slip out of tight corners like an eel. Bradford's eyes narrowed as he thought about the near-riot that closed CANPAIGN-75. And now we have another disastrous consequence of another project master-minded by Huntley. And again he is conveniently absent when the shit hit the fan. Bradford shook his head. "Christ, I can't be sure who my friends are any more."

What the hell an I going to do? He looked at the letter again and the 5-figure cost of one night's stay in La Fiesta Inn. What a fiesta! Well, the first thing to do is to answer LaLime's letter:

WINCHESTER-THORPE SCHOOL
James T. Bradford, Headmaster

January 22, 1976

Mr. Gordon LaLime
La Fiesta Inn

Dear Sir:

I am in receipt of your letter of 1/20/76 in which you claim damage to your motel due to the untoward behavior of the Winchester-Thorpe students. Because of the extent and gravity of the alleged damage, I am turning the matter over to Winchester Thorpe's firm of attorneys, Nelson, Frazier, & Gowen. I am also alerting the school's insurance carrier, Syndicated Of Boston.

You may anticipate an immediate visit by a representative. Thank you for your cooperation.

Sincerely,
James T. Bradford

"Well, that will hold LaLime for a while until we go and see whether he's trying to euchre a whole brand-new motel out of this damage claim. Now, the next thing to do is to find out who among the seniors started this drunken debacle. There had to be one or more ringleaders. By God, somebody's going to pay for this, and I'm going to find out who if I have to interrogate every damned kid in the senior class. I'll throw his ass out of W-T and make damn sure he never gets into another school. . ."

The senior class had anticipated Bradford's reaction to their Cunningham spree, and they had secretly agreed to stand together as a group in accepting the blame, thus making it impossible for Bradford to single out an individual culprit. John O'Connor cautioned Bradford against a witch-hunt type of investigation and warned the Headmaster that it might be necessary to punish the entire senior class.

But Bradford again ignored O'Connor's wise advice and pressed on with his search. He began the questioning, in alphabetical order, of every member of the senior class. The first inquiree was David Allen, Valedictorian, all-around athlete, the boy voted "most likely to succeed", known for his frank honesty and his mature attitudes. Bradford was counting on this first interview to reveal the truth.

The Headmaster ushered Allen into the office with smiling courtesy. Allen seated himself and confidently faced Bradford across the polished desk.

"Dave," Bradford began in a low-key casual tone, successfully masking his anger, "I am investigating the night of damage at La Fiesta Inn. I'm counting on you for some honest answers."

Allen remained silent, ignoring his cue to respond. He looked at his questioner eye to eye and waited politely to be asked something.

"Did you drink on the trip to Cunningham Collegiate?" Bradford queried.

"Yes, sir, we did," Allen replied, resolutely keeping to the seniors' secret pact.

"Don't you know that drinking on a school trip is against the rules at Winchester-Thorpe?"

"Yes, sir, we do."

Who supplied the booze?"

"We did, sir," confessed Allen, exactly according to the plan.

"You know the seniors are supposed to serve as models of behavior for the lower forms?"

"Yes, sir, we know."

"Then why did you abrogate your position?"

"We were celebrating the team's victory, sir."

"With what?"

"With champagne, sir."

"Who furnished the champagne?"

"We all did, sir."

"Dave, look at this desk and tell me what you see."

Allen looked wonderingly at the flame-like red grain of the coco-bolo wood and said, "It looks like a fire, a blaze with tongues of flame. Unusual."

"Well, that's a picture of how I feel about the night you seniors trashed La Fiesta Inn, fired up about finding the ring-leader who provoked that outrageous devastation of the motel. I may appear cold, but the flame is there. I won't quit until I find the lout. Tell your classmates that. Also tell them not to bother asking me for letters of recommendation to colleges or universities or job openings and the like. I cannot honestly recommend any of you until I find the one I could never approve or sponsor."

"Yes, sir," said Dave Allen, looking dismayed.

"That's all, Dave. Please tell Jimmy Appleby to report here."

Bradford continued to interrogate other seniors, but his questioning yielded the same unified "we'uns" response.

He felt angry and frustrated, but he still pressed on, becoming even more determined to penetrate the seniors' group answer. With the investigation getting nowhere, the Headmaster's grillings became a joke among the seniors. In their eyes he took on the image of an overly suspicious vindictive southern sheriff who treated every passer-by as a potential criminal. The seniors greeted one another with "Y'all're in a heap o'trouble, boy!"

The Headmaster painstakingly moved down the list of seniors and came to Ian Sunderland-Smith. By this time, Bradford had dropped his low-key approach and openly expressed his increasing anger.

"All right, Ian, you drank booze during the Cunningham trip and broke the rules of Winchester-Thorpe, right?"

"Yes, sir, we did." Sunderland-Smith answered arrogantly.

"Goddamit, forget the "we" business. Did you supply the booze?"

"Yes, sir, we did," answered Ian, boldly facing Bradford's anger.

"Isn't your family in the wine business?" Bradford insinuated.

"Yes, we are. Look, Mr. Bradford, if you want to blame or punish anyone, you'll have to expel the whole senior class."

"I might just do that!" said the Headmaster through his clenched teeth.

After his confrontation with Sunderland-Smith, Bradford was more determined than ever to single out a violator of the school's rules and hold him up as an example to the whole student body. His investigation finally came down to the last name on the senior roster -- Hardin Winchester. Bradford knew that this was his last chance to break the seniors' story. He was now desperate enough to use any means to conclude the investigation, preferably with a bang, not a whimper. Bradford brought Winchester into his office and angrily confronted him. "Look, Hardin, let's skip the polite pussy-footing and the senior flim-flam. I want to clear up this goddamned mess."

"Yes, sir." Hardin began to feel uneasy, threatened by the Headmaster's piercing eyes and angry voice.

"Didn't you organize the CANPAIGN TRAIN TO CUNNINGHAM?"

"Yes, sir, I did, with the help of Mr. Huntley."

When Bradford heard Huntley's name, he again remembered the disastrous conclusions of both CANPAIGN-75 and the great train ride. Since he had started looking into the motel mess, Huntley had not even appeared at his office door; in fact, he was almost a missing person. Bradford turned back to his interview.

"Hardin, don't you therefore have to assume some responsibility for the trip? It was originally your idea."

"Yes, I do," Winchester agreed reluctantly.

"Since you are the number one student leader, don't you also have responsibility for the conduct of other students?"

"Yes. I do,"

"You bear a respected name -- Winchester, the same as our school. Now, I want you to realize how low that respected name has fallen. Here. Read this letter from Gordon La Lime, owner of the vandalized wreckage that was once La Fiesta Inn."

Bradford handed Hardin the letter and watched as he read. Hardin's uneasy look changed to one of shock, and his face paled. He said, "God! I can't believe this much damage!"

"Believe it!" replied Bradford. "Our attorneys and insurance people have checked it out. It's as bad as it sounds. Worse, actually, because the motel will be closed for repairs at least a month."

"I went to bed, and I didn't realize. . ."

"Who furnished the booze, Hardin?"

"Did you drink yourself?"

"Well. . . yes, sir."

"You didn't try to stop it?"

"Well, sir, I. . . I voiced an objection."

"But you didn't actually stop it?"

"No, sir, I didn't."

"Don't you realize that you could have and should have? You, son of the school founder, president of the senior class, Secretary of the Student-Faculty Senate and author of its service programs, top leader of the whole school -- you could have done the right thing, But you didn't. You failed!"

"I'm afraid I did, sir."

"You failed your class, you failed your school, you failed your name, you failed your family, and worst of all, you failed yourself. Winchester, you are an utter and complete failure. It really doesn't matter who furnished the forbidden drink. You more than anyone else are responsible for Winchester-Thorpe's disgrace. Do you know what that means, Hardin?"

"Yes, sir, I think so." Winchester was swallowing hard and holding back tears of fear and anger.

"You are expelled, effective immediately. I will arrange for your transfer to another school, whichever one you choose. Of course, I will write the highest recommendation for you. That is all."

"Thank you, sir," Hardin said softly as he left the Headmaster's office.

Hardin Winchester's palms were sweating, and his knees were

wobbling under the emotional hammering he had received. His expulsion made him feel actually disconnected from everything, not just the school or family, but from life itself. It was hard to keep his balance as he went slowly down the corridors of Dawson Hall, one hand on the wall, a stunned look on his face. When Hardin's classmates heard the news of his expulsion, they immediately staged a loud protest. They formed a convoy of their automobiles and drove in a repeated circle around the campus, honking horns and yelling "We want Winchester". However, Ian Sunderland-Smith (old double-ass, as the students called him) still did not go to the Headmaster and confess that he alone had provided the booze for the ill-fated all-night party.

With the shouts of his friends ringing in his ears, Hardin went to his car and drove off the campus slowly and quietly. As he drove toward his home, he cried bitter tears of despair and rage. At the same time, he was almost overcome by the need to break the terrible news to his parents.

Back in the Headmaster's office, Bradford sat alone, also in tears. The motel damage disaster he had handled, but he was not happy with the results

He regretted having started his witch hunt, and he knew that he must face the consequences of his action. He feared that he would soon face the same fate as Winchester.

"What a goddamned mess I've made!" exclaimed Bradford.

## CHAPTER 8

# WINCHESTER-THORPE
# SANS WINCHESTER

$A$s Hardin Winchester drove toward his home, he was still in shock, staggered by his abrupt dismissal from Winchester-Thorpe, even confused and bewildered about the reasons for his expulsion. He thought about how quickly and disastrously his life had changed. In a few swift hours he had gone from president of the student body and leader in the busy rewarding life of the school which bore his name to an outcast, a zero, a nothing. This is what a convicted criminal must feel like. Was he a criminal? He was certainly convicted. When he turned down the street toward his house, he suddenly realized that this was the last time he would travel between his home and the school. He bit his lip, squinting his eyes, holding back the tears.

Hardin steered his car slowly into the driveway in front of his home. His shaking hand turned off the ignition key. In utter silence he leaned back in the seat, trying to brace himself for facing his parents. He knew it would be grim -- tears from his mother, a raging outburst from his father, shock, recrimination, threats, and regrets. He dreaded the scene to come.

Hardin took a deep breath, got out of the car, and walked slowly to his front door. When he entered, his mother greeted him cheerfully; she was not surprised at his early arrival. She was used to having him at home during the day when he had a free period.

"Hello, dear. When do you have to be back at school?" His mother asked innocently.

"Mother, I'm not going back to Winchester-Thorpe -- ever," Hardin answered in a forced voice.

"Are you finished with classes already?" she questioned.

"No. I've been expelled," he blurted out suddenly.

His mother stared at him in disbelief and noticed the tears welling up in his eyes. She hugged him tightly and started to cry softly with her head on his shoulder.

At that moment Winchester's father came out of his study. His tall figure filled the doorway, casting a giant shadow into the room, sending a chill of fear through Hardin.

"What's going on, Hardy?" his father asked, wrinkling his thick eyebrows and fixing his narrowed eyes of the two of them.

Hardin's mother turned and said bluntly, "Win, Hardy has been expelled from Winchester-Thorpe."

"What the hell for?" his deep voice roared in anger.

"Drinking on the train trip," Hardin quickly answered.

"Were you the only one who drank?"

"No, sir."

"Were you the only one expelled?"

"Yes, sir, but someone had to take the responsibility, and I failed," Hardin answered, trying to justify what had happened to him.

"Bullshit!" snapped his father with increasing anger.

"I know who has to take the responsibility for the whole goddamned mess. It's that idiot, Bradford. How the hell can he blame you?"

The senior Winchester's anger turned into a rage. He vowed to fire Bradford and withdraw his financial support from the school. His pride was deeply hurt by his son's expulsion. He shouted, "Bradford can't do that to my boy! I built the goddamned place."

Hardin Winchester, Sr. and Stephen Thorpe had, in fact, built the school thirty years ago. Both of them had grown up in the oil fields of Texas and Oklahoma and were self-made oil men. Early in their careers they had established themselves as expert petroleum engineers and had formed their own consulting firm with headquarters in Houston, Texas. As their fame spread both nationally and internationally, wealth came quickly with it.

Winchester and Thorpe then had looked around the Houston community for a project in which to invest some of their fast-accumulating funds. They bought a thirty-five acre tract of land on the outskirts of the city. The site was thickly overgrown with sage and juniper and medicine brush. In the center stood a solitary dark brick building, windowless, cracked, and crumbling with age and neglect. It was an abandoned Baptist elementary school which had become defunct long ago. When they surveyed their newly acquired property, Winchester and Thorpe looked beyond the nightmarish present and dreamed of a future in which a tree-shaded campus was dotted with the finest buildings and facilities for educating boys. It would be a monument to their own accomplishments and a training ground for young prospective engineers.

They shared the vision of a school which would rival the best Eastern prep schools in both financial support and educational excellence. With the complete renovation of the old Baptist building and the hiring of a headmaster and ten teachers, 75 students, in grades nine through twelve, were carefully screened and chosen. Thus the Winchester-Thorpe School for Boys was born.

Over the next 30 years, Winchester and Thorpe masterminded a development plan in which their school mushroomed in size from the original 75 to 700, and the program grew to include boys in grades 1 through 12. Ground was constantly being broken for new buildings.

Winchester and Thorpe ambitiously began the school's expansion by donating two and one half million dollars to build the Science-Mathematics Quadrangle, a complex of facilities that included a planetarium and sophisticated laboratories. This project was followed by the Library-Study Center with a 50,000 volume library. Then came the Fine Arts Center with a large acoustically-perfect auditorium. The latest construction was the new gymnasium completed in 1973, housing a Olympic-size heated swimming pool.

The campus now had the look of a posh country club estate, from the long tree-lined boulevard-like driveway and the sculptured grounds to the copper-roofed colonial-brick buildings carefully matched in architectural design. Winchester-Thorpe now not only had the finest facilities, but among educators enjoyed the reputation of being one of the leading independent schools in the entire country. Both Winchester and Thorpe were pleased with the progress and the status of their brainchild.

However, Winchester Senior was not resting on the oars until he had seen both of his sons graduate from his school. Frank, Hardin Junior's older brother, had graduated from W-T five years ago, but he had not distinguished himself as a student. He had gone on to college but had dropped out after his freshman year. Hardin, on the other hand, had shown both academic and athletic promise in his early years at Winchester-Thorpe. His father was proud of Hardin's accomplishments and expected him to have a brilliant future, beginning with his early acceptance at Harvard.

Winchester now saw the dream shattered and his son's future imperiled. He was bitterly angry and would not accept such an unreasonable dictum from that fool of a headmaster. His fight against Bradford had just begun. He paced the floor, his face red with rage. His wife tried to calm him down. "Win, please don't get too excited. Watch your blood pressure," she cautioned.

"The hell with my goddamned blood pressure!" he roared. "I'm more concerned about getting rid of that ass-hole Bradford!"

Hardin had never seen his father so blazingly furious. A wave of guilt feelings washed over him. With his head bowed, Hardin turned his back on the wrathful scene and retreated to his room. He flopped himself down on his bed and stared blankly at the ceiling where an old chandelier hung on a heavy wrought-iron chain from its center.

He had always throught the long curved arms of the fixture looked like spider tentacles, and that the whole thing, which was made of rough black wrought-iron, took on the look of a gigantic black-widow spider hanging from its web in an attack position, ready to seize and devour its prey. He remembered how he and his brother Frank used to swing on the chandelier, like Tarzan on a jungle vine, sometimes both together to see which one could hang on for the longer time. How silly they must have looked, both of them dangling their feet in the open air like monkeys. And the old light fixture was pleanty tough; it never broke or let them down.

Hardin went from reminiscences to regrets as he thought about his brother's school career and present Bohemian-like life style. Frank had slid through Winchester-Thorpe without much work or effort, had flunked out of college, and then had hitched to Colorado where he had become a hanger-on and sometimes instructor at a ski lodge. Hardin knew that his father was wholly disappointed with Frank and had now put all of his hopes in Hardin's future. But he too had let his father down -- he was expelled. He had failed his responsibilities. He was no better than Frank. Worse. Hardin cried bitter tears of frustration with himself. He began to feel drained from the emotional turmoil he was enduring.

As he fell into a troubled sleep, the blankness that slowly engulfed him became a nightmare, a black hole into which he fell headlong, helpless, hopelessly trapped, condemned to the black hole of failure for as long as he remained alive.

In the dead of night, Hardin suddenly snapped wide awake. He was thinking clearly and knew exactly what to do. He turned on the light, sat down at his desk, and hastily wrote a note. Then he placed his desk chair directly under the iron chandelier. He removed the thick black leather belt from his slacks and carefully measured his neck. He stood up on the chair and fastened one end of the belt to one of the black iron legs of the spider, leaving a noose running through the belt buckle. With his neck in the noose, he kicked the chair away with his long strong legs.

The next morning Hardin's mother arose early to prepare his favorite breakfast, French toast and ham steak. As she turned down the hall toward his room, she wondered why his bedroom light was already on; usually, she had to awaken him in the morning and turn on the light herself. She pushed the door wide open, and her glance got as far as his pendant legs which cast a grotesque shadow on the wall. Her scream was long, seemingly endless, the kind that raises the hair on the neck and turns the skin to goose-flesh. Death had come in the night but had not left alone.

Her scream seemed as if it were continuing in the throaty shriek of the ambulance as it carried away the cold body.

Hardin's funeral service was entirely private, attended only by family members. Then a shroud of silence fell over all the Winchester-Thorpe community as they grieved their devastating loss.

## CHAPTER 9

# THE BOARD OF TRUSTEES

The shrill ring of the telephone broke the gloomy silence of the Winchester home. As Mrs. Winchester walked toward the jingling, she felt relieved to have contact with somebody outside of her own grief-stricken world.

"Hello," she answered. . .Just a moment, please. . ." She called to her husband, "Win, it's Steve Thorpe."

Hardin Winchester Senior sat alone in his darkened study where he had spent the past month in brooding silence since his son's death. He was overwhelmed by all-consuming grief, as well as deep-seated anger at the people and circumstances involved in his boy's self-destruction. Winchester had frozen himself into a state of inactivity, shutting himself off from his friends and his business. He reluctantly reached for the telephone.

"Hello, Steve," he answered in a somber tone.

"Win, I'm sorry to bother you, but I need to find out if you've changed your mind about resigning from the Winchester-Thorpe Board of Trustees."

"No," Winchester answered shortly.

"Look, Win. I need you. The school needs you. Won't you consider coming back to us?"

"Steve, you and the school don't need me. Maybe, my money," replied Winchester, striking out at his old friend.

Thorpe refused to respond to the angry insinuation. Instead, he said quietly, "Win, I think I know the depths of your despair. After all, Hardin was almost like a son to me. I knew him so well that I'm certain that he would not have wanted you to cut yourself off from the school. He loved it too much."

Winchester said nothing for a long moment. Thorpe's words had penetrated his shell of grief and forced him to really think about Hardin and why the boy had chosen to end his life. Win's thoughts turned to the note which Hardin had written before he died that night:

Dear Mom and Dad,

I'm deeply sorry to leave you like this, but I don't see any other way to end the mess I've made and to save our family from having a complete failure on its hands, which is what I am.

Dad, whatever you do, please don't turn your back on Winchester-Thorpe. The school needs you to survive.

Goodbye and all my love.

Hardy

Winchester swallowed hard and wiped the tears from his eyes. He resumed talking with Steve Thorpe.

"All right, Steve, I'll come back under one condition -- that we get rid of that lame excuse of a headmaster, that son-of-a-bitch Bradford."

"Consider it done," Thorpe answered decisively. "Remember, Win, Bradford works for us. We run the school -- and the Board of Trustees as well, as long as we two stick together."

"I know," Winchester affirmed.

"Win, the spring meeting for the Executive Committee of the Board of Trustees is scheduled for next Tuesday. We can take care of Bradford and a few other problem people then. "You'll be there?"

"Yes, Steve."

Winchester hung up the phone and sat back in his desk chair, feeling relieved to end his period of mourning and to join again the outside living world. This was the only way in which he could avenge his son's death. His eyes narrowed as he thought about Headmaster Bradford. "Oh, yea," he muttered to himself, "we will take care of Bradford. I'll certainly see to that."

Time, which had once seemed to stand still under the paralyzing shock of young Hardin Winchester's death, now went racing by. Tuesday, the day of the Board meeting, came quickly.

At the Winchester-Thorpe School, Bradford sat alone in his office, facing a pile of correspondence and paperwork. He pushed the paper aside and tried to focus his thoughts on the Board meeting that night. He knew that the agenda would include a review of the faculty in which he would be put on the spot to answer both for his colleagues and himself. He felt like a criminal who was about to stand before a tribunal. He was deeply disturbed by feelings of guilt triggered by Hardin Winchester's suicide. Of course, that made him even more apprehensive about facing the Board members. Would Hardin Winchester Senior be there? A confrontation with the man would be hell. A dreadful evening.

Tuesday, in the early evening, Winchester eased his black Cadillac onto the wide ribbon of freeway which described a long straight line disappearing abruptly into the skyline clutter of downtown Houston. He aimed his car toward the Republic Bank Building which dominated the horizon, Winchester and Thorpe had a luxurious suite of offices on the 43rd floor. They shared this premium space only with the Petroleum Club, an exclusive bar and restaurant whose customers were the wealthiest and most powerful tycoons of Texas. During the long cocktail hours many eight and nine digit deals were consummated in which Winchester and Thorpe often played key roles.

As Winchester approached his traditional seat of power, he felt a renewed sense of control which he had almost lost during his month's absence. The quiet and deliberate speed of the bank tower's elevator seemed to emphasize this feeling as Winchester was swiftly lifted forty-three stories and delivered to the main door of his offices. As the sculptured bronze door brushed across the thick gold carpeting of the outer lobby, Winchester heard voices coming from the main conference room. He reached for the oversized bronze door knobs and opened the heavy carved walnut doors. He surveyed the long rectangular room with its sumptuous rare-wood paneled walls lighted by elaborate brass sconces. Then he focused on the persons seated on either side of the wide polished walnut conference table.

The faces were familiar. Not only did these fellow board members form the close-knit circle of power in Winchester-Thorpe, but also they controlled the business community of Houston. Here was a collection of powerful figures, each presiding like a czar over his own financial empire. There was Vincent Campbell Sr., heir to the Campbell Soups fortune. His $2,000 dollar donation to the school's CANPAIGN had helped his son's freshman class to win the competition. Over there was Ian Sunderland-Smith, Sr., the wealthy owner of a large international network of vineyards. His son Ian had provided the champagne which had turned the school's train trip to Cunningham Collegiate into a disaster.

Winchester greeted everyone and sat down at one end of the conference table. He left the space at the table's head for Thorpe who was Chairman of the Executive Committee. He had just settled in place when the doors opened, and Thorpe appeared. Stephen Thorpe crossed the threshold of the room at his usual halting pace. He walked dragging his right foot and leaning heavily on a carved ebony cane with an ornate silver handle. His limp was a constant reminder of his days as a wildcatter when a fall from an oil derrick left him with a shattered right leg. Thorpe was short in stature, just over five feet tall. However, his weathered face, broad shoulders, and big rough hands showed his great strength and his years of hard physical work. Outside of his leg, he was in top shape, as well as being strikingly handsome. His black neatly-cut hair was brushed with gray at the temples and accented his tanned angular face. His most compelling feature was a pair of clear light blue eyes whose cold stare could inspire fear and at the same time could command respect.

Thorpe took his seat at the head of the table and immediately called the meeting to order. His cold blue eyes appeared to soften as he looked at his old friend Hardin Winchester Senior seated at the other end of the table.

"Welcome back, Win," he said softly. The other members smiled and nodded in agreement.

"The agenda of this meeting," Thorpe announced formally, "calls for our review of the performance of some faculty members of the Winchester-Thorpe School and for an evaluation of the Headmaster. Bradford will be here in just a minute."

Almost at that moment the members heard the click of the outer door. James Bradford appeared suddenly on the threshold of the conference room and said in a nervous cracking voice, "Good evening, Gentlemen."

Thorpe directed him to a chair against the wall near the chairman's end of the table. He was not permitted to sit at the table itself. No one was seated in that circle of power except the chosen few. From the foot of the table Winchester stared at Bradford like a rat snake at his prey. His mind was filled with thoughts of revenge. "I'm going to get that stupid bastard, and nothing can stop me," he said to himself. Bradford was very aware of Winchester's unremitting deadly glare; he shifted in his chair with unease, turned his head away, and looked down at the floor.

Chairman Thorpe produced a folded paper from his suitcoat's inner pocket and broke the tense silence. "Gentlemen, we are here to review with Mr. Bradford the performance of certain faculty members at our school."

Bradford knew that the names of Thorpe's paper were the "hit list" of the Board and that some teachers' heads were destined for the chopping block. He stiffened in uneasy anticipation of the tense discussion in which he would be called upon to defend some of his colleagues and justify his continued use of them. He knew that both he and certain teachers were under fire.

"Let's begin with the chaplain, Henry Prescott," Thorpe said. "I think we need a real Episcopal priest, not a defrocked one. Have you any comments or suggestions?"

They came in rapid succession:

"I'm told that he uses profanity and questionable language in class."

"He's an alcoholic. He always has a drink in his hand."

"Yeah, at every party, he's first to arrive and last to leave, unless the liquor runs out."

"He was supposed to supervise the students overnight when at Cunningham, and look what happened to the motel. Where in hell was he?"

"He was in a bottle somewhere. That's where he was. That's where he always is. We ought to get rid of him."

Bradford's face grew flushed as he heard all the negative comments about Prescott. He knew that they were based on truth. He had counseled the chaplain about his foul language and heavy drinking, but his advice had fallen upon deaf ears and a closed mind.

Bradford cleared his throat and said to the group, "Chaplain Prescott works very well with students. He successfully handled CANPAIGN 75, a great community service project for the school."

"You're wrong again," Winchester answered abruptly. "It was Huntley who actually ran CANPAIGN and made it a success. I agree with Steve. We need to get rid of the bastard."

The executive Committee members nodded their heads in agreement.

Their long serious faces together formed a grotesque Goya-like reflection on the highly polished surface of the dark walnut conference table. They are like Spanish Inquisitors, Bradford thought, condemning heretics out of hand.

"Next is Kenneth La Croix," Thorpe said, his list in hand. "He seems to be the "angry young man" type."

A chorus of comments rattled around the table:

"He's a sophomore who never grew up."

"He wants to take on the system -- any system."

"He likes to stir up the kids with rebellious ideas."

"He was with Prescott supposedly supervising the students that night when they trashed the Fiesta Inn. Where the hell was he?"

"He's a poor example for the students of Winchester-Thorpe."

La Croix was disposed of by a unanimous thumbs down. Exit the eternal sophomore.

"How is Bruce Lindsley doing in his first year, Bradford?" Thorpe queried.

"He's doing fine," Bradford answered and then unfortunately added, "the kids love him."

"I hope he's not loving them back," Winchester commented sarcastically. "Is it possible to find a normal French teacher?" "He is usually either a wimp or a queer or both."

Bradford winced at the sharp criticism of Lindsley. The young teacher was a handsome cherry-cheeked fellow with slightly effeminate mannerisms and a total lack of interest in athletics. He looked like a student himself. However, Lindsley was an excellent teacher who demanded top performance from his students.

"I don't want to have my kid taught by a fairy," Sunderland-Smith said emphatically. Bradford was aware that Ian Sunderland-Smith Junior had received a well-deserved failing grade in Lindsley's French class. The father had made a loud protest, but both Bradford and Lindsley had refused to change Ian's failing grade.

"I don't think that we should renew Lindsley's contract," Winchester suggested. He took pleasure in countering Bradford's positive comments, another way to strike back at him. The Board members again nodded in agreement and destroyed the career of a young promising teacher.

Thorpe turned to Bradford and dismissed him with, "That's all, Mr. Bradford."

The Headmaster stood up and quickly left the inquisition chamber. He was bitterly unhappy with what were obviously prearranged decisions to dismiss Prescott, La Croix, and Lindsley. They were three of his strongest teachers, but they were controversial enough to fall victims of the Board's machination. Now he, as their supervisor, had the disagreeable task of firing some of his best teaching talent. He felt sure that his own head was next on the chopping block.

The Executive Committee resumed its meeting as Bradford closed the door behind him.

"What shall we do with Headmaster Bradford?" Thorpe asked the talking heads around the table.

"He's got to go!" Winchester pronounced and banged his fist on the table. "The kids don't like him, his teachers don't trust him, and he's doing a piss-poor job on running our school. He's got about as much good judgment as a scared skunk."

A barrage of negative criticism poured out of the group:

"He's an impulsive hothead."

"The faculty is organized against him."

"His wife Betty is a hopeless alcoholic."

"He behaved like a maniac in the investigation of the train ride episode."

"He doesn't get along with O'Connor."

"He takes all the credit, but Huntley does all the work."

Thorpe closed the discussion saying, "We cannot forgive nor forget what Bradford did to Hardy Winchester. However, I suggest that we give him enough rope to hand himself by the end of the school year. After commencement, we'll dump him, and without recommendations to any other school."

Everyone agreed with Thorpe. Faces disappeared from the table top. Dust and silence crept back behind the great carved doors.

CHAPTER 10

# THE NEW SCHEDULE

J. Robert Huntley III had deliberately avoided contact with Headmaster Bradford since Hardin Winchester's death. He wanted to escape even the slightest appearance of blame or responsibility for that tragic episode. He quietly allowed Bradford to take all the heat (after all, that was his job, wasn't it?) while Huntley's record of successes and triumphs remained unblemished.

Huntley immersed himself in his busy workaholic world. One of his projects grew out of Bradford's request for a research of modular scheduling, the latest cutting-edge approach to building a school's master schedule. In this system, class periods became modules which could and should have varying lengths according to the instructional demands of each course in the curriculum. Since the construction of a master schedule becomes an intricate mosaic of varying modules, a computer is needed to fit the modules together.

Huntley plunged into work on this project, conducting meticulous and exhaustive work in the various phases of modular scheduling. He read countless journals, interviewed several schoolmen who had recently installed the modular system, and surveyed several computer companies who were offering to build master schedules with this latest technology. Finally, Huntley concluded his research, wrote up the results, and was ready to confer with the Headmaster. One morning, a week after the Executive Committee's spring meeting, Huntley appeared at Bradford's office door as the clock bonged 8:00 A.M. He caught Bradford just as he arrived in a semi-slumberous state.

"Good morning. Brad," Huntley said cheerfully. "May I see you for a few minutes?"

"Sure, J. R..." Bradford answered with half-open eyes. "Come on in and have a seat. I'm going to get some coffee to wake me up. Would you like some?"

"No thanks." Huntley went into the sanctum sanctorum as Bradford headed down the hall to the faculty lounge.

Bobby Huntley sat on his fat rear and relished his surroundings here in the secret world of his ambitions. He again admired the over-stuffed red leather chairs, the wide flame-grained polished cocobolo-wood desk. "Some day. In the not-too-distant future, I shall occupy that chair," Huntley muttered to himself. He was tempted to try the desk chair in Bradford's brief absence, but he thought better of doing that, since he didn't want to be seen by anyone, least of all by the Headmaster himself.

"It won't be long now," Huntley continued to himself. He knew that Bradford was in trouble. With his own efforts and the help of the Gourmet Supper Club, the faculty was turning against Bradford. And the Board of Trustees, he knew, was blaming Bradford for young Winchester's suicide. Huntley was confident that he was a good step closer to taking Bradford's place. Soon he could bring those secretly-printed headmaster name cards of his out of hiding.

Bradford returned to his office, alert with caffeine, his eyes open and interested. "What's on your mind?" he asked, rousing Huntley from his reverie.

Huntley replied, "Brad, about a month ago, you asked me to do some research on modular scheduling. Here are my findings." Huntley handed over a thick clear-fronted binder which contained a detailed typewritten report.

"Looks very impressive," Bradford commented. "Again, you've done the job in your usual thorough and matchless manner. I'll read this tonight after dinner."

"Thank you," said Huntley. "I think that we should invite a computer company to acquaint our faculty with modular schedules. In fact, I'd recommend giving the students a day off so that we could arrange an in-depth study of the concept. This could be an in-service meeting for the teachers."

"Great idea!" Bradford replied enthusiastically. "Let's jump on it right away, if you can line up the participating computer outfit."

"No problem there," Huntley assured him. "I can set up a date with M.I.S.S. -- Modular Instructional Scheduling Systems -- right away."

The next day, a memo appeared in the faculty mailboxes:

Friday, March 8, 1976

TO:      All Faculty

FROM:    James T. Bradford, Headmaster

SUBJECT: In-service Faculty Meeting

On Friday, March 15, all classes will be canceled so that we may conduct a day of in-service training. The subject will be modular scheduling. We will meet in the auditorium at 9:00 A.M. Everyone must attend.

J. T. B.

This memo produced a barrage of critical remarks from the faculty:

"How the hell can he cancel classes without consulting us?"

"Who want to know about the modular crap. There's nothing wrong with our present schedule."

"Beware the Ides of March."

"He's probably invited some computer gurus to bore us all day. Maybe I can catch up on my sleep."

"At least we get a break from the little monsters, and a long week-end. Perhaps we'll finish up early."

"Maybe we will get a decent lunch for a change."

"Modular, bodular, codular. Who gives a shit? We will keep on teaching the same old way, no matter what."

On the Ides of March all the faculty filed into the school auditorium wearing their usual bored and cynical expressions as if pre-determined to shut their ears and their so-called minds to everything they would hear that day. They secretly enjoyed the break in their routine but would never admit it. They also resented having to listen to an "expert" from "outside".

"Good morning, everyone," Bradford said cheerfully. "It is my pleasure to introduce to you Dr. Harvey Birnbaum and Dr. Stuart Bailey from M.I.S.S., Modular Instructional Scheduling Systems. They will tell us about modular scheduling and other computer applications in education."

The attention of the faculty was riveted on the two men who stood before them, mostly because of the unusual physiognomy of the two experts. They were alike and yet unlike one another. Both had dark swarthy complexions and balding heads. Both obviously had excessive body hair; their faces showed dark stubble even though they were clean-shaven, a "five o'clock shadow" at nine o'clock in the morning. Coarse black hair at the neck line spilled out over the collars of their white shirts.

The backs of their hands, and even their fingers, were so heavily haired as to look like fur.

But there the resemblance ceased. Harvey Birnbaum was a short man, just over five feet tall. His brachycephalic head on a short neck, his wide mouth and large white teeth, all lent him a primitive anthropoidal look. His arms were unusually long for his height, and it was easy to imagine his walking on his knuckles like one of Tarzan's great apes.

In sharp contrast to Birnbaum, Stuart Bailey was a tall slender man over six feet in height. His thin arms dangled loosely from wide broad shoulders. His suitcoat hung like a sack over his long torso and made him appear to have no waistline. He walked awkwardly, his arms loose, almost like a puppet. His face was oddly round with heavy high-set eyebrows. He wore thick horn-rimmed glasses which magnified his eyes. His whole face constantly carried a look of surprise.

Bailey was the first one to speak. "I am Stuart Bailey. This is my partner Harvey Birnbaum. We want to talk to you today about modular scheduling and computer applications in education."

As Bailey spoke, Birnbaum was lumbering around the speaker's platform in the front of the auditorium. On a display table, he placed an empty cardboard box on it side. The box had no top, and the exposed inside showed a divider which separated it into eight equal-sized compartments.

Bailey pointed to the box and said, "This box represents your master schedule which is now divided into eight 45-minute periods per school day. We don't want you to be <u>boxed in</u> by your own schedule." He chuckled himself and waited for a similar response from his audience. He didn't get it.

Kenneth La Croix reacted with a muttered comment -- "Christ, this is the Birnbaum and Bailey circus for children in the center ring." O'Connor added in a low voice, "It's a three-penny opera with two cents change."

Bailey continued to speak, unaffected by a lack of response. "You can also divide your day into four ninety-minute periods." At that point Birnbaum removed the first divider and replaced it with another showing four large equal compartments.

"Or you can go to a truly modular division with periods of varying length within the school day." Birnbaum replaced the second divider with still another which contained a number of unevenly-sized compartments which fit perfectly in the box. Bailey raised his arms in triumph as the modular divider slid into place.

"I don't believe this," commented Henry Prescott, trying to focus his one good eye on Birnbaum and Bailey. The rest of the faculty looked on the simplistic performance with equally incredulous eyes.

Bailey then launched into a long elementary lecture about the history of computers in the field of learning. His voice was unfortunate, a monotonous nasal drone which soon became a soporific for the teachers. Heads began to nod, and in a short time the entire group became engulfed in a slumberous fog. Bailey droned on interminable like some distant stream burbling over its well-worn pebbles. Even when his voice finally ceased, no one stirred from the restful siesta until Bradford stood up and wakened the audience in time to render thanks to Birnbaum and Bailey for their somniferous presentation. Everyone had awakened in time for lunch.

On the following day Bradford conferred with Huntley and then decided to use the services of M.I.S.S. on a trial basis. A week in this spring term would be set aside to run through a modular schedule. Huntely easily convinced his friends on the faculty to go along with the experiment. He consulted with each teacher about the preferred length of the module for each class. He then devised an "A" through "E" cycle representing the five individual days of the school week with recommendations for the placement of classes in the cycle. Finally, Huntley mailed his prepared information to M.I.S.S. so that they could design the trial schedule.

The faculty lounge buzzed with gossip and wisecracks about the intrusion of Modular Instructional Scheduling Systems into the teachers' private world.

"Will it be hit or a MISS?"

"I am simply MOD about this whole irregular MISS."

"Will popcorn be served at the next performance?"

"Do you like your classes long and loopy or short and sweet?"

John O'Connor announced that he had written a new song for old

Winchester-Thorpe, so the faculty barbershop quartet got together and sang it to the tune of "I'll Be Seeing You":

> We'll be MISSing you
> In every shortish-longish day
> When Birnbaum-Bailey start our play
> And we get used to things that way
> We'll miss the bell for every class
> Before the week is through
> We'll be running off our ass
> As we'll be MISSing YOU.

The teachers sang lustily as they waited in anticipation for the trial run of modular scheduling.

# CHAPTER 11

# THE TRIAL RUN

In mid-April a large heavy package arrived from Modular Instructional Scheduling Systems addressed to J. R. Huntley III, Director of Studies, Winchester-Thorpe School for Boys. Huntley smiled as he read the label, noting that his name and title were precisely accurate. In his imagination the Director title was blotted out by that of Headmaster. His tongue played over his thick lips as if he could taste his ambition physically as he thought about his final step up to the pinnacle of his academic world.

The opened package contained a thick computer print-out about the size of a Manhattan telephone directory. Huntley found it difficult to decipher the computer codes of the instructions. However, to his relief he discovered orderly schedules for each teacher and each student in the grades 9 through 12 of the Upper School. He immediately set about separating the scheduling for faculty and for students. He had to distribute this information within a period of only two days.

Huntley gave out to the individual teachers the modular schedules which corresponded exactly to their requested time demands. Teachers of Advanced English were given the longer class periods which occurred every other day and which allowed time for students to complete lengthy reading assignments. The Social Studies teachers were allowed two forty-five minute lecture periods followed by a ninety-minute period for showing a film. The Mathematics and Foreign Language teachers in their conservative mode were granted the traditional forty-five minute sessions for their day-by-day lessons. The Science teachers were the most pleased with their schedules which allowed for the completion of extended experiments within ninety-minute periods. The teachers were so happy with their trial schedule that no one questioned the noticeable gaps of unscheduled time in the academic day.

Monday and Tuesday of the trial-run week went by very smoothly. Both students and teachers seemed to follow the varied time modules without a problem. However, on Wednesday, the experiment began to unravel. John O'Connor stationed himself, as usual, in the hall between classes. He enjoyed exchanging greetings with the students; at the same time his observant senses could detect a problem almost before it happened. That day, the students seemed more animated, or agitated, than normal. The usual din in the hallways was more deafening, the voices more strident.

Vincent Campbell, Jr. approached O'Connor with schedule in hand. "Where do I go now, Mr. O'Connor?" he asked.

O'Connor examined the computer-generated schedule and found it difficult to follow. Once he had figured out the varying times, he was able to direct Campbell to his next class. In the process of studying Campbell's schedule, O'Connor's eyes had fastened on Friday and discovered that the only subject class booked for that day was Mathematics at 8:00 A.M. The rest of the periods were a series of study halls interrupted only by the lunch hour. O'Connor's jaw tightened as he wondered how many more student schedules were like the one he had just seen. He spotted a group of seniors huddled in a corner. In the center, Ian Sunderland-Smith was showing his schedule and laughing as he pointed to it.

O'Connor went straight to the group and spoke sharply to Sunderland-Smith. "Ian, please let me see your schedule."

"Yes, sir, Mr. O'Connor," the boy answered in a well-rehearsed voice full of faked exaggerated respect.

O'Connor snatched the schedule out of Sunderland-Smith's hand and was not surprised to find another Friday full of study periods. "Thank you for your invaluable help, Ian," he said sarcastically as he returned the schedule, spun on his heel, and headed for Headmaster Bradford's office. He felt like a stranger who was about to invade a foreign land. He had not visited Bradford's office in months, not since the headmaster had indicated that he was not welcome, nor was his advice. The only communication between the two of them was by terse official memos. When he knocked on the open door, Bradford looked up in obvious surprise. "May I see you a minute?" O'Connor asked formally.

"Sure, J.L.," Bradford answered, motioning with his long arm for O'Connor to enter. "I'm glad to see you," he added warmly. For months Bradford had hoped for a reconciliation with his friend and former mentor. Perhaps this would be the opportunity to mend their broken relationship.

"Brad, we have a serious problem with the modular schedule," O'Connor began. "Too many students have too much unscheduled time on Friday. If we don't intervene, this place will be a zoo with all the monkeys out of their cages." He explained the anomalies he had found on the schedules he had checked.

"Sounds serious," Bradford said. "Let's get together with Huntley immediately after dismissal today."

"Fine," O'Connor agreed. "We have to head off this disaster."

That afternoon, O'Connor and Huntley were filling the big red leather chairs across from Bradford's desk, waiting for him to open the discussion.

"Well," the Headmaster began, "The Mod Squad is at it again. Maybe we should simply cancel what few classes there are on Friday and schedule cookies and lemonade all day. Have a real chocolate chip freak-out."

The three men laughed together, clearing the tense air.

"What the hell went wrong?" asked Bradford.

"Huntley responded, "Brad, I think that the computer programmers simply forgot to put the study halls into the scheduling cycle," Huntley's quick explanation was a cover-up for his own oversight. He was the one who forgot to include study periods in scheduling recommendations to MISS. Later, when he realized his error or omission, he submitted a list of study halls without specifying the days they were to be scheduled. He had hoped that MISS would distribute them throughout the week's cycle. But they had not, of course; hence the egg he was scrubbing off his face.

"We have no choice other than to redo the schedule for Friday," O'Connor stated. The sooner we begin, the sooner we'll be out of the woods." The others nodded in agreement.

Since all the student schedules were filed by class years, the resulting mountain of papers which had to be examined and changed looked almost insurmountable. So the three administrators decided to divide up the job and work individually; Huntley would reschedule the Seniors, Bradford the Juniors, and O'Connor the Sophomores. They went to work in their individual offices and agreed to stay until the schedule changes were completed. They would do the Freshman class together since it was the easiest to schedule.

Four hours went by quickly. Bradford became so absorbed in the task that he forgot to call Betty to tell her that he would be very late. At 8:00 P.M. the three men assembled in Brad's office. For the next two hours, they compared notes, made some adjustments, and together took care of the Freshman class sessions. When they finally finished, they were pleased with one another and the job they had done. They had never before worked so well together. Bradford felt that once again he had a functioning administrative team. "Maybe there is some hope for me after all," he muttered to himself as he locked his office and walked out of Dawson Hall.

As he stepped out into the open air, the darkness surprised him. It must be late. His pace quickened as he headed for home. He knew that his wife did not like to be alone at night. His busy career with its supervisory problems, its board and faculty meetings, its public relations, its parental complaints, had consumed all of his time. Bradford fully expected Betty to be angry, even hurt, about his lateness and his failure to call her. He sensed that her reaction would be a cry for help from her solitary world. He hoped that she had not turned to the bottle. He dreaded facing her.

# CHAPTER 12

# AFTERMATH

When Bradford stepped into the entryway of his long spacious ranch-style home, he heard the strains of "Beautiful Dreamer" played with loud sour discordant notes on their baby-grand piano. He hated the song, and Betty knew it. She played it only to irritate him when she was angry. She was, in fact, a skilled pianist who had turned down a scholarship to Juilliard School of Music; instead, she chose to marry Bradford and follow him through his career.

He opened the front door, and Betty struggled to her feet and stood unsteadily clutching the piano and waving at him with a glass of bourbon. "Jimmy Wimmy, I am sooo glad to see y'all," she said in an exaggerated fake southern accent. "Would my beautiful dreamer like a little old drinkie-poo?"

"Betty," Bradford began in a disappointed tone, "you're on the sauce again. I thought that you promised to stop."

"Empty promises, empty bottles, empty days, they're all the same," Betty replied, flourishing her glass and sloshing Wild Turkey over the piano keys. "I'm an alcoholic, and you're a workaholic. Isn't life grand?"

"Betty, I'm sorry that I've neglected you, but I've been so very...."

"Busy, busy, busy." Betty cut short his apology. She had listened to the same excuse so many times before that she refused to hear it again. "Jimmy, you've been such a busy beaver that you don't even have time for other little beavers. I've got a furry little beaver right here who is anxious to see you," she coaxed in a playful tone, reaching down to pull up her skirt. But she lost her balance and fell to the floor in a drunken sprawl, her head narrowly missing the piano bench.

Bradford rushed to her and found that she had completely passed out. He picked her up, carried her to her bedroom, gently undressed her, and tucked her in bed. He studied her, still a beautiful girl, as she lay sleeping with an utterly peaceful expression on her lovely features. He fought back the tears as he thought about her hopeless alcoholism. He knew that drinking had become her escape from loneliness and unhappiness.

Bradford stepped into the long hall and headed for his study. He needed to rest and think and recover from the tensions of the day. Before he sat down, he went to the liquor cabinet and took out a bottle of Courvoisier brandy and a snifter. Then he reached into his carved wooden cigar humidor and extracted a long rich Havana cigar. Finally, he settled into his soft cloud-like leather chair, carefully lighted his smoke, and took the first aromatic sip of his drink.

His thoughts tumbled through the day which had just passed and the school year which will have passed in a couple of months. He remembered the disastrous end of CANPAIGN-75. Then there was the ill-fated train trip to Cunningham Collegiate and the trashing of La Fiesta Inn. Bradford winced with guilt feelings as he thought about Hardin Winchester's suicide. And right now is the fiasco with modular scheduling. Even though he, O'Connor and Huntley had repaired the Friday schedule and staved off an impending mob scene, he knew that the faculty rumor mill would be buzzing with news of the near disaster which many would regard as still more proof of the headmaster's ineptitude.

Bradford's eyes narrowed as he focused his thinking on J. Robert Huntley III who seemed to be the mastermind behind CANPAIGN-75, and the Great Train Ride, and the MISS schedule. All these projects had brought "trouble, and more trouble," to Winchester-Thorpe. But when the trouble starts, Huntley can never be found; he's an expert in dodging censure or culpability. Bradford had also heard rumors about Huntley's leadership in the Gourmet Supper Club, a group of dissident faculty members who had aligned themselves against him, the Headmaster. Well, O'Connor had warned him about Huntley's ambitious motives, but he had refused to listen; maybe he should have lent an ear. No, it doesn't do to become too paranoid about rumors and rumblings among the faculty. He would begin to lose confidence in his ability to be Headmaster of Winchester-Thorpe.

In the silence and seclusion of his study, Bradford admitted to himself his almost overpowering fear of failure. His fear was a learned response from his childhood. His father had pushed him to excel in everything, leaving no tolerance for being even second best. Now, as an adult, Bradford was still working to please his father. His thoughts turned bitter about the distinct possibility that he might be losing control of himself, his marriage, and his job.

Bradford was wakened from his reverie by the striking of the grandfather clock in his study. He sat up as he realized that it was almost midnight. He remembered that he had left a pile of unsorted papers and unanswered mail on his office desk at the school. He felt compelled to go back there to take care of this paperwork and to organize his priorities for the next day. Unconsciously, Bradford was trying to sort out the mess he had made of his life. He was tired, angry, and even fed up with life itself. He stood up in protest and stormed out of his home. He slammed the front door of his house behind him and crossed the dark campus in long strides.

*     *     *

James T. Bradford was found dead the next morning. He lay stretched out on the long couch under the picture of President Truman. O'Connor discovered the body; he had come early to the Headmaster's office to check final arrangements for Friday's schedule. O'Connor worked swiftly to effect the removal of the body before students and teachers arrived for the school day. The ambulance came and went, and doctors arrived at the Headmaster's home to sedate Betty and take her to the hospital. O'Connor closed and locked Bradford's office and went swiftly back to his own where he reached for the telephone. He dialed Steve Thorpe's number and waited.

"Steve," he began, "this is J.L. O'Connor. I'm afraid that I have some bad news for you. Headmaster Bradford died last night."

After a long pause, Thorpe blurted out, "What the hell happened?"

"I found him in his office when I arrived about 7:00 A.M. I'm not sure of the cause of death, but it must have been a heart attack or a stroke."

"I'm sorry to hear that," Thorpe said with genuine regret. "What are we going to do for the rest of the year, J.L.?"

"I don't know," replied O'Connor. "This is why I called you first thing."

"Why don't you and Huntley run the school for the rest of the term?" Thorpe suggested decisively. "We can take care of naming his successor formally after this crisis is over. Okay, J.L.?"

"Yes, we can handle it, I'll talk to Huntley right away."

"Thank you," Thorpe said. "I'll see you later."

O'Connor went directly to Huntley's office. He entered and closed the door behind him. Huntley noted his visitor's grave expression and wondered what was wrong.

"Bradford is dead," O'Connor explained in a tense voice. "He died last night in his office, apparently of a heart attack or stroke. ."

"What!" exclaimed Huntley, genuinely shocked. "What do we need to do?"

"I have already spoken to Steve Thorpe, and he asked that you and I run the school for the rest of the term. Is that all right with you?"

"Of course," Huntley replied. I'll do whatever it takes."

In that moment Huntley put aside his selfish ambitions and was ready to help O'Connor and the school in the heat of this crisis.

"We need to have a school meeting," O'Connor said.

"I'll set the meeting for this morning and get the word out immediately," Huntley replied, grabbing his telephone.

At 8:15 A.M. the students and faculty assembled in the auditorium. The crowd buzzed with excitement, wondering why the special assembly. As John O'Connor approached the microphone, the audience hushed in respectful silence.

"Students and faculty of Winchester-Thorpe. I have sad news for you. I regret having to tell you that Mr. Bradford, our Headmaster, is dead. He died last night in his office. The doctors believe that he suffered a massive heart attack."

Students and teachers sat in stunned silence. They could not believe what they had just heard. Slowly, whispers of realization spread through the house.

"I need to tell you that Mr. Bradford loved the school and you, its students and teachers," O'Connor continued. "Mr. Bradford was a teacher here himself several years ago and then returned to become Headmaster. He worked tirelessly to better the school. We all owe him a debt of gratitude. Let us have a moment of silence."

Every person bowed his head in silent tribute to James T. Bradford who was now as silent as they and profoundly at rest.

"Now for some daily instructions," O'Connor said, getting the group's attention again. "You are dismissed to go home for the remainder of the day. There will be no classes tomorrow in memory of Mr. Bradford. Faculty, please stay for a few minutes after the students leave."

The students filed out of the auditorium in solemn silence. They were shocked by the sudden mortality among them. Even students who did not like Bradford as headmaster were saddened by the death. The faculty moved forward and seated themselves in the front rows.

"Colleagues," O'Connor addressed them, "we are in a crisis mode at Winchester-Thorpe. Somehow we have to pull together to complete the school year. I know that many of us have had our differences with Bradford, but now is the time to put those aside and focus on the future of this great school. Mr. Thorpe, of the Board of Trustees, has asked J.R. Huntley and myself to direct the school for the rest of this term. We need your cooperation and support to bring this school year to a successful close. Will you help us?"

The faculty was positive, and most of its members verbal, in agreement. They were moved by his plea for their help. Everyone left the meeting with a renewed commitment to Winchester-Thorpe and a determination to finish the year.

CHAPTER 13

# THE FINAL ASSEMBLY

The faculty was true to its promise to O'Connor. All of the teachers exerted their best efforts to finish the school year on a positive note. The Gourmet Supper Club was dissolved, and the divisive atmosphere disappeared from Winchester-Thorpe. Even the morning coffee in the Faculty Lounge acquired a cheerful taste. The rest of April passed without incident, and the school launched itself into its concluding month of May. The faculty busily prepared for the crowning events of the year, the Final Assembly and Commencement.

Everyone had genuinely rallied around the common cause of Winchester-Thorpe; everyone, that is, except J. Robert Huntley III. His common cause was himself, but he thought it political to conceal his ambitions and to play the busy loyal servant during this interim. Huntley's dreams as the man-who-would-be-king were shared by his wife Margaret. She was even more ambitious and conniving then Huntley himself. More than anything she wanted to be the Headmaster's wife. She coveted the social status and privileges attendant to that position.

Late in the afternoon of the first Monday in May, Margaret greeted her husband at their door with a special gleam in her eyes. She wore an exquisite black cocktail dress by Givenchy which clung to her chubby body like a second skin. Huntley smiled as he smelled "Gardenia-Passion" perfume by Annick Goutal of Paris, a scent which she wore only for their seductive encounters.

"Margaret, darling," he laughed, "you've been dreaming again about our little secret."

"Yes, I have." Margaret smiled as she handed him a vodka martini created and chilled to perfection. "Who do you think will be the new Headmaster of Winchester-Thorpe?" She asked knowingly.

"The best man, of course," Huntley asserted confidently with a wide grin on his bearded moon face. He reached into the vest pocket of his suit and handed her a white business card, the kind he had been concealing in the locked drawer of his desk.

Margaret read the card aloud. "J. Robert Huntley III, Headmaster, Winchester-Thorpe School for Boys. It looks exactly right, dear. Soon everyone will know who is the best man for the job."

"Yes, Margaret," Huntley explained, "and why not? I am the most likely candidate. After all, I graduated from Winchester-Thorpe, and at the top of my class. I know the school well, both as a student and as a teacher. Look at my record of accomplishment for this year." He was referring to his position as Director of Studies and President of the Student-Faculty Senate. Both positions allowed him to exercise his organizing skills. He was proud of his role as mastermind of CANPAIGN-75 and the Great Train Ride. He blithely ignored the riots and vandalism sparked by those events.

"What about O'Connor?" Margaret asked.

"No, the Board of Trustees won't appoint him," Huntley said in a matter-of-fact tone. They all know that Bradford and O'Connor hated each other. Besides, who was Bradford's right-hand man this year?"

"You were, darling," Margaret answered quickly. She was excited and even sexually aroused by their talk of power politics. She reached for her husband's face and kissed him longingly. Her tongue slid between his lips and traced a circle inside his mouth. She suddenly pulled away and stood up. "Time for another drink," she declared as she darted into the kitchen to prepare more vodka martinis. When she returned, they began a series of toasts to their mutual success as Headmaster and Headmaster's wife. The drinks had not dulled their sexual appetites. Soon they both stood up and headed for the bedroom.

They were both aroused and tore clumsily at each other's clothing. As Huntley penetrated Margaret's plump pink thighs, she dug her long polished fingernails into his flabby back, spurring him on. She kept gasping in his ear, "Oh, my master . . . my headmaster, ooh. . ." With each word Huntley drove himself deeper inside her until they both arched into a thundering mutual orgasm. From the climax they fell into a deep sleep, keeping themselves in their own warm private world.

So, as the days of May slipped by, J. Robert and Margaret worked at keeping their ambitious dreams alive, with a little help from sex and martinis. Their daily happy hour was devoted to Huntley's upcoming promotion to Headmaster and their further prospects for glory in his future career. They talked about having to move some day -- perhaps to New Hampshire when Huntley might become Headmaster of Phillips-Exeter; or to Massachusetts where he could possibly head Andover; or to Wallingford, Connecticut for him to take over Choate Rosemary Hall. Of course, he could maybe wind up near Philadelphia at Germantown Academy or the Episcopal School. But first he would have to break into the headmaster ranks by his appointment as Head of Winchester-Thorpe. And that was in the bag. J. Robert and Margaret were unshakingly convinced of that.

In late May the day of the Final Assembly arrived. Both faculty and students looked forward to this special community event. Students would be rewarded for their achievements, and the faculty would be recognized for the excellence of its teachings. This year would provide special excitement: a new Headmaster would be named. Who would it be?

On the morning of the Great Day, J. Robert Huntley III was up at the shiver of dawn to prepare for the most important event of his career. First, he disappeared into the bathroom and locked the door. He did not want Margaret to see him shave off his beard. He had made his own decision to change his image, to wipe out even a hint of the hippy style he had affected, and to adopt a more conservative appearance. No more dirty gym shoes, no more motto tee-shirts, no more crummy blue jeans, no more scruffy whiskers. The Board would see a beardless, neatly-trimmed Headmaster dressed in the best of taste, suave, mature, and managerial in manner.

As he hacked away at his beard, Huntley practiced his acceptance speech which he would deliver today when he was appointed Headmaster:

"Ladies and Gentlemen, Members of the Board of Trustees, Colleagues, Parents, Students, I am deeply humbled and grateful for the opportunity to serve you as Headmaster of Winchester-Thorpe School. I pledge to do my very best to uphold the standard of excellence which is the hallmark of this great school. I very much appreciate your trust and confidence in me. Thank you."

Huntley was pleased with these conventional sentiments calculated to have just the right convincing effect on the conventional audience. In his imagination he heard the hall thunderous with applause for their stalwart leader who would guide them through the remaining years of the 70's and into the next decade. Of course, by the next decade he would likely be gone, having accepted a more prestigious position in one of the top-ranking preparatory school of the country.

Huntley's broad clean-shaven face was smiling as he came out of the bathroom and went to his wardrobe chest to select his costume for the day. He laid out a dark charcoal-gray suit which he had purchased at Brooks Brothers for this special occasion. He then selected a dark red power tie which would go perfectly with the suit. He put on a lightly starched Oxford cloth pin point button-down shirt. Next he slipped his feet into calf-length dark gray socks and a pair of brand-new black

Bali shoes from Switzerland. After donning his suit and tie, Huntley stepped out onto the flagstone patio adjacent to the bedroom's French doors. He scuffed the leather soles of his new shoes on the rough paving; he wanted no slips when he mounted to the stage to receive his appointment. He returned to the bedroom and looked at himself in the cheval mirror. Looking back at him was the perfect image of a perfect headmaster.

The Final Assembly was due to begin at 1:00 P.M. By 12:30 the auditorium was almost full. Huntley and Margaret were seated in the front section reserved for faculty and administration. On the stage, J. L. O'Connor was seated with Steve Thorpe and Hardin Winchester Sr. O'Connor was Master of Ceremonies for the affair. The audience hushed as he arose and approached the microphone. "Ladies and Gentlemen, Students, Guests, and Friends, Welcome to Final Awards Assembly for the 1975-76 school year. While we are here to recognize the achievements of our students, we want to dedicate this assembly to the memory of James T. Bradford, our late Headmaster." Everyone bowed his head in a moment of silent tribute.

The program that followed was a long drawn-out series of award presentations which became eventually tedious and tried the audience's patience and attention. Each department chairperson gave out awards for outstanding work in his discipline. In English, there were book prizes named after Harvard, Yale, Princeton, and Brown Universities. In Mathematics and Sciences, there was the Rensselaer Polytechnic Award for the most promising student in those fields. In Foreign Languages, there were prizes for the most accomplished student in French and Spanish.

When the time came to award the prize in History, O'Connor announced, "This year, we have a new History award in memory of Mr. Bradford. As most of you know, he taught Advanced Placement United States History. This year's James T. Bradford History Award goes to Tom Bradley, an outstanding history scholar who is in the junior class of our school."

The audience thundered in applause, the students whistling at Bradley's recognition. They knew that he had been Bradford's protege and loyal disciple, with access to Bradford's primary sources for his research papers. The students recognized Bradley's closeness to Bradford by calling him "Brad", also the nickname of his mentor. As Bradley walked in long strides toward the podium, O'Connor thought, "He even walks like Bradford." They shook hands warmly, for they had developed a close relationship. Bradley was an excellent student and an accomplished athlete; O'Connor had taken him under his tutelage and had become a second father to this outstanding young man.

The Assembly continued with the awarding of prizes for the best actor and the most accomplished musician in the Fine Arts Department. Then came the athletic awards, the longest and most boring part of the program. Each coach for every sport from water polo to dry fly casting felt obligated not only to recognize the most valuable player but also to describe in detail the events of the past season. The one saving moment of these awards was when Hardin Winchester Jr. received posthumously the award of Athlete of the Year. Hardin Sr. accepted the award for his son.

O'Connor again stepped up to the microphone for the concluding event of the Final Assembly. "It is my pleasure to present to you Mr. Steven Thorpe, President of the Board of Trustees and Co-Founder of the Winchester-Thorpe School."

"Thank you, J.L.," Thorpe said warmly. "I bring to you important news about the future of our fine school. I am here to announce the name of the next Headmaster." J. Robert Huntley III stiffened in his seat, and he shuffled his feet preparatory to rising. He wore a pasted-on smile which covered the tension he was feeling deep in his gut. His memory was scanning his acceptance speech.

"I am both proud and pleased," continued Steven Thorpe, that the next Headmaster of Winchester-Thorpe will be. . ." He paused for dramatic effect, and the audience seemed to hold a collective breath. . . "John L. O'Connor." Everyone stood up and continued to clap, whistle, yell, and cheer. They were expressing not only their approval of the choice but also appreciation for O'Connor's many years of long loyal service to the school.

Instead of delivering a lengthy extravagant acceptance speech, O'Connor spoke a simple heart-felt thank-you. He would show in action rather than in words what he would do for the future of his beloved school.

Huntley and his wife sat stunned, hardly believing that the name they had heard was not his. The band began to play the school song, and people started to get to their feet and gather in groups for excited talk. The Huntleys spoke to no one. They slipped quietly away through a side door of the auditorium and returned to their faculty lodging. J. Robert locked their front door and then deliberately ripped the telephone wire off the wall. With his face pale as a full moon from the loss of his beard and his Headmaster job, he sat down at his desk and wrote this note:

May 29, 1976

To:    Steven Thorpe
FROM: J. R. Huntley
     Sir:

I RESIGN.

J. R. H.

Suitcases packed, J. Robert Huntley III and his rosy-thighed upwardly-mobile Margaret folded their tent like the proverbial Arab and silently stole away. They were gone before midnight, disappeared, vanished completely, and were never seen again at Winchester-Thorpe or in Houston or even in the state of Texas.

# CHAPTER 14

# EPILOGUE

The year was 1982. Six years had passed since the appointment of John O'Connor as Headmaster. When he had first taken over, it was as if a pall of mephitic fog had suddenly been blown away by a fresh and wholesome wind of change, and the Winchester-Thorpe School had begun to flourish as never before. Academic outcomes improved as teachers and students worked with their administration in a climate of trust, respect, and total cooperation. Everyone took pride in being a member of the community of Winchester-Thorpe. O'Connor had become loved and respected by both the faculty and the student body. His presence was felt in the day-to-day operation of the school. He seemed to be everywhere and know everything.

One day, as he made his rounds during the varsity sports period, he stopped at the Olympic-sized swimming pool attached to the modern expansive gymnasium. He opened the large glass double doors. Through the misted air he heard the voice of the swimming coach barking gruffly, "You're in more fog than the Newfoundland Banks.

Pick up the pace. Come on now," he urged. "Reach, pull, kick, reach, pull, kick. . ." He increased the cadence, and the swimmer responded by stroking and pushing his way to record time on the next lap and down the pool. "Good job!" The coach said as he extended a hand to the swimmer and pulled him out of the pool.

O'Connor moved toward the voice and recognized Tom Bradley, the new swimming coach. How is it going, Brad?" he asked. He had at first felt a bit awkward addressing Bradley as "Brad", a nickname formerly used for the deceased Bradford. However, since Bradley reminded his of Bradford, he was becoming more comfortable with the new "Brad".

"It's going well, Mr. O'Connor," Bradley answered, showing his respect for the Headmaster whom he would never think of calling by his first name.

Bradley was an excellent example of the new breed of teacher that O'Connor was attracting to Winchester-Thorpe. Bradley, like his late mentor Bradford, had gone to Harvard, majored in History, and had become an All-American swimmer. At the urging of O'Connor, Bradley returned to his old preparatory school to teach History and coach swimming; he felt good about doing so since he felt as if he owed much to the school for what it had done for him.

Bradley was enormously popular with the students. He was a master story-teller who held his history classes spellbound with his tales and anecdotes. His knowledge of history was encyclopedic, and his teaching was woven through with lessons from the legendary past. He was an avid sports fan. His history quizzes always contained an extra-credit item, such as "Who hit the winning home run in the World Series of 1960?" With Bradley, history ceased to be as dry as dust. It was even occasionally wet with tobacco spit from some history-making baseball player. Bradley was becoming a master teacher.

O'Connor left Bradley at the pool and made his way across the campus to Dawson Hall. On his way, he thought about Bradley and knew that he had one of the "right ones" for Winchester-Thorpe, an exceptional outstanding and successful teacher. As O'Connor reached his office and sat down in the high-backed swivel chair and looked at the autographed picture of President Truman, still on the office wall, he thought of Jim Bradford and how he, too, had a brilliant beginning as a history teacher and swimming coach. But he had chosen to give up teaching and take on the busy hectic life of a headmaster. He had been eaten alive by his choice.

O'Connor promised himself that he would guide young Bradley and try to protect him from the same fate. He would nurture the teaching genius of Bradley and any other talented young teachers. This was his life's pledge and mission.

As O'Connor leaned back in the chair, he almost felt Bradford's presence. When he closed his eyes, he imagined seeing Bradford's face wearing a smile of satisfaction. It was the expression of a man finally at peace with himself.